Annihilate: Space Apocalypse Book One

ANNALISE CLARK

For all my girls who dare to love while the world is burning.

Acknowledgment

Cover design by Pixie Covers
Thank you, Lizzie, for bringing my visions to life and giving faces to the characters who live in my head. Your covers are works of art.

Join Clark's Coven – FB Reader Group
Thank you to everyone who has been there since the very beginning, offering support, reading my early works, and helping spread the word. You're the reason I keep writing.

Shoutout to Jennifer and the Bitchy Bookworms – Here are your "spicy lesbians in space". Enjoy!

CONTENT WARNINGS:

Loss of a parent (not very detailed, just a memory in passing)
After-effects of war
Explicit sexual content

CHAPTER ONE

The whole galaxy's gone to shit and in this dog-eat-dog world, you do what you must to stay alive.

That's how the two of us became partners. The only female bounty hunters left in space, and the best in the business, we came highly recommended and high on the hit list of every thief, pirate, and vagabond up to no good on this side of the galaxy.

Hunting down the Galaxy's Most Wanted kept food in our bellies and our ship in the skies. But all that time on the run, chasing the bad guys to make ends meet can get lonely. So, when a new species moved onto the planet we now call home and try to take over the remaining human survivors, we fight back.

It's time to annihilate!

As for how we became lovers... well, that's another story. But if you'd like to hear it, take a seat and make yourself at home.

"Safari, get over here!" Kavita called to me from the front of the ship where she had been navigating us toward the Tiberius Terminal for our next assignment.

Her robot dog, Memory, followed at my heels as I made my way to the cockpit. His eyes flickered and his voice warbled, as it always did when he was calculating something. That little guy and his brilliant computer mind had saved our asses on more than one occasion.

"Good boy," I whispered, stepping through the threshold and into the pilot area of our little ship. She was a bit worse for wear after our last job, but she got us where we needed to go. And we'd just dumped most of our savings into building a new house on Logara and staking down roots for the first time since shit hit the fan after the war, so we'd need to complete this job to do some repairs on the ship before taking another.

If things settled down, we had dreams of watching the two suns rise over a mug of hot coffee on the patio like the good old days when humans lived on Earth. But this job... well, there would always be a need for bounty hunters.

No matter how good things got in the galaxy, someone would always be looking to shake things down or take what they didn't earn. And as long as there were bastards out there thieving and destroying what wasn't theirs, you'd find bounty hunters like us chasing them down and dragging them back to justice.

That's not to say I'm on the side of the government either - if you want to call them that. No, our leadership since the war had been questionable, at best. But at least there was some sort of governing happening.

Goddess knows, the people can't govern themselves! They'd all but proven that in the last decade of lawlessness. After the Red Sun Order had attacked the galaxy and entire planets were blown to smithereens or burned in the wake, we'd had to rebuild where we could and how we could.

I was only 21 years old when it started, but I've been on my own a lot longer than that. Unlike many who lost their families in the war, I lost mine long before that. My home planet? Well, *that* I did lose in the war, but I'd been desperately trying to get off that rock since I was a teen, so I suppose it was just as well.

Neither Kavita nor I had started on Logara. In fact, we'd not even known this little blue planet with the golden suns existed until we came here a few months ago on a mission. We were on the tail of infamous space pirate Harley 'The Sparrow' Swien when one of our informants tipped us off that The Sparrow had been spotted on a small planet inhabited by human survivors of the war.

We snatched his ass up and hauled him in to collect our bounty but vowed to come back to Logara and have a better look around. Three days later, we decided that after years of exploring one end of this galaxy to the other, Logara was as close to home as any place we'd seen so far. Pooling our money, we purchased a plot just outside the main city limits, and construction of our home was set to be complete in two months.

It was exciting, if not a little scary, too. I'd never been the settling down type. Meeting Kavita changed a lot of things about me. And although I wasn't ready to give up the bounty hunter life completely, I was excited about our new home on Logara.

Things moved a bit slower on Logara, but that

was part of its charm for us. Whipping our little beat-up ship from planet to planet, hunting the worst scum of the galaxy was profitable but exhausting work. If we had a quiet little place to call home, we might even take a vacation now and then.

I was pulled out of my thoughts by what she had called me to the front of the ship to see.

"What the hell is that?" I muttered, staring out the front glass toward the Amazone Station. The space station where we were to land was covered in large, mechanical spiders that seemed to be breaking down the docking areas.

"Fuck if I know but it doesn't look good." As our ship hovered in space, pausing its trajectory toward the destination, we watched the white and grey spiders violently rip pieces of the docking station apart. Debris floated out into the darkness, but we weren't yet close enough to better assess the situation.

And I didn't intend to get any closer.

Neither of us had seen mecha like this since the war. We'd thought they'd all been destroyed after the Red Sun Order was stripped of their power. There were plenty of robots around – hell, some planets were completely inhabited by them, but none of them were quite like these. There had always been something a bit more intense about these.

"Plan B?" she asked, glancing my way, and redirecting our flight path. She always knew what I was thinking before I said it out loud, which was part of what made us such good partners.

"Aether Base?" I guessed, and Kavita nodded her agreement. The Aether Base was neutral territory, and it was close enough that we could make it on what little fuel we had left in the ship's tanks. We could refuel there and try to figure out what the fuck was happening at Tiberius Terminal.

If there was anything I had learned after ten years of bounty hunting and flying ships, it was that you never went in blind and that situations can always change without warning. Whatever those spiders were doing, and whoever had sent them, we weren't going to fly into a hot mess without knowing the facts.

And so, we charted a path to our Plan B, and with Kavita flying manual in the cockpit, I went back to assess our inventory. We'd been running low on food and supplies on the way here, too, and I had a connection at Aether who might be able to hook us up. Supplies were scarce, but he owed me a favor, and this might be the perfect time to collect.

CHAPTER ONE

Toward the back of the ship in our sleeping quarters, my wolf Zion lay resting on one of the cots. I patted the gentle giant on the head as I passed by. Despite his current display of docile nature, this black beast was a killer. He was also my longest and oldest friend.

Zion had been with me since I was a little girl. An orphan, born on planet Tecephus, the bastard daughter of a poor migrant mother who was murdered by space looters years before the whole planet would be destroyed in the war. He was the only thing I had left from my old life, my home planet, or of my mother.

He had been just a pup back then when they sent me off to an orphanage I would quickly escape from when they told me I couldn't keep Zion. In the first few years after I lost my mother, I felt deep loneliness. Sometimes, it threatened to take me over completely. In time, and with Zion's companionship, I had learned to accept my fate in life.

For years, I believed I was destined to be alone. I was strong and independent, and I wore it like a badge, determined to prove I didn't need or want anyone else. Refusing to wallow in my misfortune in life, I used it to propel me ahead through all of life's challenges. With Zion at my side, I knew I could achieve anything I set my stubborn mind on.

Running from the orphanage meant I had to lay low – at least until I was of legal age, and no one would try to force me into the enslavement they called the foster care system. The first big decision I ever made on my own was to leave my home planet.

Everyone on Tecephus knew me. They knew what had happened to my mother. And they seemed hell-bent on reminding me constantly. When I ran away with Zion, I'd heard how they *tsked* when they spoke of me, how their noses turned up in the air, how they narrowed their eyes. They'd called my mother "trash" and thought me just the same.

I'd never much cared what anyone thought of me or said about me, however. To get away from Tecephus where everyone would keep trying to toss me back into protective care, I hitched a ride on a cargo ship. Zion was still small enough that I could stuff him into a backpack. Taking the very few things I owned along with us, I crawled into the back of the ship when the pilot was having a few too many beers at a local pub.

He must have still been buzzed the next morning when he took off because he never even noticed me in the back. There was a small porthole window in the back and as he took to the air and my home planet became smaller and smaller beneath us, I fell in love with the freedom of space for the very first time.

Since, then Zion and I had seen so many planets, met so many different races, and experienced all kinds of new and exciting things.

It had been just me and him in this big, wide universe. That is until I met Kavita...

CHAPTER
TWO

I could never forget the day she barged into my life, guns a'blazin. After chasing a mark to some seedy little planet in the outer ring of the galaxy, I'd finally cornered him in the back of an illegal saloon. I'd slipped the bartender a few too many of my hard-earned credits in exchange for access to the employee's area.

My informant had told me he'd be back there, waiting for his lady to be done with her shift slinging brewskies to a bunch of assholes in second-hand flight suits and 5 o'clock shadows.

Imagine my surprise when I popped through the doors, gun drawn, and came face-to-face with my bounty… being held at gunpoint by some random white woman. He stood almost a foot taller than her, but she had him back in a corner, a tall, white robot dog blocking the only other way out.

She was wearing thigh-high black leather lace-up boots, a black mini skirt, and a corset top (also black, which silver chains across the front). Her dark black hair was wild around her heart-shaped face, and I thought I caught the glimpse of a blue tint on the bottom.

Before I just stood there staring like a fool, my mouth opened and blurted out something equally stupid.

"You can't be here."

What? Even I don't know what the fuck I was trying to say.

"I mean, you need to leave now," I tried again. Annnd another miss... I was really off my game today.

"I think you're mistaken," she crooned, her voice smooth as warm honey. "I'm precisely where I aim to be."

Without moving the weapon she had trained on my mark, she shifted the one in her right hand toward me. That damn machine dog had its red eyes focused on me, too, and it felt like it could bore right into my soul.

Where was Zion right now?

My heartbeat quickens in my chest, adrenaline flooding through my body, and nothing comes out as I open my mouth to speak. It's just as well. I'd certainly embarrass myself even further.

"That's my guy," I fumbled, voice cracking, pointing toward the mark with my gun. "Let him go?"

Oh gods, it was supposed to be a command, not a question!

"Really?" she says, quirking an eyebrow and looking me up and down. "I'd have pegged you as more of a lumberjack type, but who am I to judge?"

She was laughing at me now, pure and simple. And I'm not sure I blame her, really. I was a hot mess. A far cry from the cool and collected seasoned bounty hunter who had first walked through that door. One look at this smoking hot woman and I was losing my mind.

"Wait, what? No, not *my guy*, not like that."

She barks a laugh in my direction, which only makes me even more flustered. I could feel my pale cheeks reddening from across the room. Part of me wanted to turn around and go right back out the way I came and pretend this whole damn thing had never happened.

But I needed fuel, and I hadn't eaten in days.

CHAPTER TWO

I couldn't let this woman get in my way... even if she was the most devastatingly beautiful woman I had ever seen.

"Then what's it like, Princess?" she teases.

"Okay, first off," I begin, straightening my spine and pulling my entire stature up to the full five foot three inches I was gifted with. "I don't do dudes."

There was a flash of something in her eye at that – curiosity maybe – but then it was gone as quickly as it came.

"And secondly, that's *my* bounty," I finished, pushing as much edge to my voice as I could manage, but unfortunately, still sounding a bit too mousey.

"*Your* bounty?" she laughed that same laugh again, low and gravelly. Fuck, it was sexy! Why was she so sexy?

"Ladies, ladies, no need to fight," the stupid mark spoke up then, probably hoping we would be distracted, and he could get away. "There's plenty of Billy the Kid to go around."

She smirked then and put both guns back on Billy. "About that," she nods my way as she speaks, but doesn't look at me. "I'm not into dudes, either."

Only the slightest look of disappointment on his

face as he realized his plan was crumbling as quickly as it had formed in his feeble mind.

"But if I were..." this gorgeous woman continued while I just stood there watching like a damned fool, my heart about to beat clean out of my chest. "I certainly wouldn't go for some guy with the nickname 'The Kid'."

I snort-laughed at that, but when Billy the dumbass tried to make a move, I sprang into action.

He darted to the left, but a table blocked his path. In an instant, I was there, scooting the table across the room and essentially blocking him in, to which he hopped over it and made his way toward the door I had just walked in through.

Within seconds, I was on his heels, the mystery woman and her weird robot dog were on mine. Billy ran back into the saloon, attempting to hide through crowds of people. I'm small but fast, so I was on him in a flash, grabbing him by the back of his scruffy shirt and yanking him back.

He nearly lost his footing, his arms flailing out to the sides as he balanced himself, one of them hitting the arm of a big, burly man holding a pint of beer.

The cold, frothy liquid splashed all over its owner, Billy, and myself as I tugged him back toward me, huffing loudly in the process.

CHAPTER TWO

"What the hell?" the Beer Man shouted before turning and swinging his large fist right into Billy's face. His body slumped as he lost consciousness and I fought to hold on before he fell to the filthy floor, taking me with him.

From my left, I heard squeaks and beeps of that robot dog as it came into my field of vision, throwing its body under Billy's. The dog was so tall, it came above my waist when on all fours, so Billy's body slumped over the back was still nearly eye level with me.

Crazy perfect timing!

But, if the dog was here, that meant...

And before I could finish processing the thought, the woman was in front of me, grabbing his wrists from behind the dog and slapping electronic cuffs on them.

Dammit!

In an instant, I pulled my own cuffs out and zapped them onto his wrists at the same time.

"What are you doing?" she demanded, just inches from me now, pulling Billy to his feet and off the dog's back. He was starting to come to, his eyes groggy, and a crowd was forming around us, with Beer Man looking like he still wanted to punch someone.

"You owe me a beer, bounty hunters," the Beer Man growled, as saloon security pushed their way through the mob forming around us.

Eh, shove it up your ass, I muttered under my breath. Right now, my focus was fully on Billy the Dumbass.

With both of our electronic cuffs on the mark, he was digitally assigned to both of us, which meant one couldn't claim the bounty without the other unless we resolved this issue. But none of that mattered if we all got pummeled in the saloon.

"Billy?" I heard a faint female voice call from the middle of the crowd. Stealing only a momentary glance, I realized it was his girlfriend. I'd recognized the dark-skinned, pink-haired woman from my field notes.

"Go now!" she shouted, looking directly in my eyes. My right hand was still on Billy, who was looking confused and groggy as the woman held right to him with her left hand and the robot dog pushed him from behind.

Making trouble with patrons in the saloon could get us into some serious trouble with their security – or worse, dead.

"Don't have to tell me twice," I muttered, following them as we pushed our way through the crowd of patrons and further away from the security guards.

"Go, go, go!"

Just ahead was the main door to the space saloon, a bit of the sunshine from outside seeping in through a crack in the glass, cutting through the foggy, dingy vibes inside. We were almost there. I was *not* going to let go of Billy, but the three of us running while clinging to each other was beyond ridiculous. I nearly fell twice!

"Just let him go," she sneered at me.

"YOU let him go," I fired back.

"He's *my* bounty."

"No, he's *mine.*" I insisted.

My ship was just around the corner but unless I could get her to both physically let him go, and remove her digital cuffs, I wouldn't be able to claim the bounty even if I did manage to haul him into my sole custody.

With security close on our heels, patrons of the saloon shouting and throwing things at us, we burst through the door, still attached by Billy in the middle, and nearly stumbled over as we slammed into a big dude in dark brown.

He stood well over six feet tall, towering over us and Billy, too. His large frame took up most of the doorway and blocked the suns that were setting over the horizon.

"Just who do you think you are making trouble in Saron's Saloon?" he half growls, half sneers at us, reaching one of his huge hands out to grab the woman by her right arm. Her left arm is still tightly wound around Billy's shirt.

Damn, she's persistent.

"Let her go!" I shout, slamming my fist into his right side, but he flicks me away like a gnat. I have no idea why I am demanding he release her. I should have taken this opportunity to get Billy for myself and run back to my ship, cuffs be damned. That's a bridge I could cross when I get there.

As I pick myself up off the ground, he has her in a tight grip now and I see her hand loosening from Billy as the big man from the saloon shakes her like a ragdoll. Just as it slips free, Billy starts to run, but I'm on him in a flash.

Looking back once over my shoulder, I see the woman struggling with the large man, but still somehow managing to maintain control – for now. She's tough but he's a big dude, so I hesitate ever-so-slightly before chasing after Billy. It's all the time he needs to get a few paces ahead of me.

Torn between helping her and getting my

bounty, I look back one more time and hear her shout, "Get Billy!" as she's punching the big man in the face with both fists.

Just as it looks like Billy might get away, cuffed arms and all, Zion flies into my peripheral vision and tackles him to the ground. With his hands bound behind his back and the big wolf on his chest, he's not going anywhere.

"Good try, Billy," I taunt as I approach him, "but not good enough."

I pull a leash-like device out of my pocket and connect it to the electronic cuffs on his wrists. Now he won't be able to just slip out of my grip.

"Nice work, Zion," I nod to my best friend. Then, I look over my shoulder again. She's still fighting him, but the woman seems to be tiring faster than the big man and others have come out of the saloon by now.

She doesn't stand a chance...

Letting out a loud sigh, I give my wolf orders that even I don't understand in the moment. "Zion, help her please."

CHAPTER
THREE

As I drag Billy kicking and screaming back to my ship, I trust Zion to get the woman, by any means necessary. He's helped me reel in bounties bigger than her, so I trust he can get the job done.

What I need right now is to secure this mark and get the ship ready to take off. My little Bumblebee has seen better days, and while she still takes to the skies, she sometimes needs more encouragement these days.

But she was mine, and that was something that meant the world to me – the entire universe to me. All I'd ever wanted, my whole life, was to be free. And Bumble, she gave me the freedom I needed so desperately in this life.

CHAPTER THREE

So, I didn't hold too much of a grudge when I needed to kickstart her into action, especially in desperate moments like this. She was doing her best.

"Wow, nice duds you got here," Billy teased as I loaded him into the ship and tied him into my tiny cargo bay.

"It's good enough," I grunted.

"An admiral position to take," he muttered.

I pulled his restraints a bit tighter and glared at him. "Look, Kid, you can shut up willingly, or I'll shut you up. I think you'll find the former choice a lot more pleasing than the latter."

"Whatever you say, Cupcake," he replied, but that was the last I heard out of him.

Already in the cockpit bringing the engines to a low purr, I heard the screaming as Zion got closer to the ship. I'd left the side hatch open for him, but Zion was such a big wolf, he had to duck to get in the doorway, and this time he came with a very sexy, very angry woman in his jaws making this even more difficult.

He must have bumped both her head and her legs getting her in the door and then dropped her roughly to the floor once inside, his large body blocking her only way out. Only steps behind them, I heard the shouts from the crowd at the saloon.

"I've got Billy!" I shout from the front. "Close the doors, Zion."

As he moves to obey, she begins to object. "Wait a minute, you can't kidnap me!"

"Would you rather take your chances with that angry mob back there?" I nod in the direction of them as a couple of gunshots ring out in the air.

"No," she says, picking herself up off the floor of my ship that I am suddenly feeling self-conscious about. "I'd *rather* you stay out of my way and let me take my bounty and complete my mission."

"Whelp," I say, the engines sputtering before humming to life, all systems finally go, "it looks like he's *our* bounty now, Princess. And I suggest you buckle up because this is going to be a bumpy ride."

No longer are the words out of my mouth before I slam it into gear and begin moving the old ship forward. She's tiny but mighty and I don't care much for the sound of those idiots banging on the side of her as we start to lift off.

This planet always had been full of a bunch of degenerates. No respect for anyone trying to complete an honest day's work.

I pull up hard, and the woman – who still hadn't

secured herself into my back seat – was knocked off her feet and slammed across the ship. Instantly, I felt bad, but there was no time to waste. Once I navigated my way into the sky, the ground of the planet growing further away from us, I looked back to find her sitting in the jump seat, her hand on her head.

"I'm sorry about that," I say, my voice weaker than I intend.

"I don't need your pity," she grunts from the back of my tiny ship. Her robot dog bleep-bleeps at her side.

"I'm Safari," I offer.

"I don't give a shit," she barks out, tensed in the seat, her eyes shooting daggers at me and Billy, and in all directions.

It was the longest and most uncomfortable trip across the galaxy I've ever had.

Once we arrived at the turn in location on Planet Xalara, I was fully convinced she was going to murder me when I landed, but miraculously, she didn't. Maybe the long flight in silence had given her some time to think.

"He's my mark and I will fight you for him, to

the death if need be!" She shouts as soon as we land, and the doors start to open.

Okay, maybe not...

For a brief second, I feel bad. She had technically gotten to him first. But I'm also intrigued. I've never seen another female bounty hunter before, and I've never seen a female as beautiful as her before.

I was suddenly overcome with the desire to know her name, her story, her... everything. But what I *did* know about her is that she wasn't joking. She would fight me to the death, if need be. I had to find another way.

"Look," I say, trying to reason with her. "I really need this..."

"You think you're the only one," she spits back, looking me dead in the eyes. A challenge.

"And I believe I saved your ass back there."

"Which only needed saving because *you* got me into trouble in the first place," she shouts back at me. A fair enough point.

"Okay, there has to be a solution here. Maybe we can..." she glares at me with the most stunning deep brown eyes I've ever seen. "Maybe we can work together?"

"I work alone."

"Just this once?" I practically beg at this point.

She's not removing her cuffs from Billy, but I refuse to remove mine, either. If we take him into the precinct like this, the captain will have both our asses. This isn't how Bounty Hunting works.

And with the state of the Galaxy these days, the last thing anyone wants to do is referee a couple of hot-headed bounty hunters having a spat over who rightfully owns a reward. They'd sooner shoot him in front of us and give no one anything.

"Safari? Is it?" she says, softening her tone and squinting as she looks me up and down.

"Yes."

"You owe me a ride back to my ship."

"I'd be happy to," I smile. "As soon as I collect my bounty so that I can refuel."

"Uugghhh," she groans, not even trying to be quiet or polite. "You are such a pain in my ass!"

"The feeling's mutual, Princess."

"Stop calling me that," she scolds.

"I would if I knew your name." If I couldn't kill her with kindness, maybe I could annoy her to death.

"Kavita," she says with a sigh.

Kavita. Such a beautiful name.

"Kavita," I start, choosing my words very carefully. "Can we call a truce and help each other out, just this once? Let's turn Billy over, split the reward, and I'll escort you back to your ship, free of charge."

She appeared to be chewing on the words, the taste bitter on her tongue, but finally, she reluctantly agreed.

And that was how it all began.

I wish I could say we became the best of friends and lovers right after turning Billy in and splitting the bounty but that's not quite how things went down. It would take more than that for Kavita to warm up to me, and for me to ever consider trusting anyone other than Zion in this life, but it's safe to say that first meeting had a huge impact on the both of us.

CHAPTER FOUR

PRESENT DAY

As soon as we arrived at Aether Base, it was apparent we were not the only ones who had run into trouble at Tiberius Terminal. The whole space station was buzzing about it before we'd even fully pulled the ship in to dock.

Kavita pulled our baby in to the nearest docking station, after getting permission from the sky jockeys, and I was grabbing some of our water canisters before she'd gotten completely out of the cockpit.

Memory had tapped into the news frequencies on the space station trying to get intel. Zion looked at me and then at Kavita as she made her way over to me. He cocked his head to the left, and she answered him with a smile and a pat on the head.

"Things are crazy out there and this is a neutral base. You best stay here so no one thinks we mean trouble."

"And we need you to keep an eye on Athena," I added, moving instinctively to my tiptoes to kiss Kavita as she scooped an arm around my waist and lower back. Zion always did as I told him, but he could make my scent from miles away and if I so much as let loose an anxious fart, he'd be there in a heartbeat.

Named after the Greek Goddess herself, Athena was our ship, and our home. Pooling our money from the sales of our previous ships, we'd made our relationship official when we went all-in on her from a scrap yard on Illinope.

She barely ran, but Kavita saw something beautiful in her bones, as we worked our fingers to the bone, along with the help of Memory to rebuild and reprogram her before putting her back into the open skies. Working on Athena together had brought us closer together than we'd ever been. It may have taught me a few new curse words I hadn't known existed, too.

Like her namesake, she was strong, knowledgeable of war, and full of wisdom. I'd painted a large owl down her starboard hull. On the other side, beautiful olive trees, snakes in their branches. This warrior goddess had carried us from one side of the galaxy to the other many times over by now. She never let us down.

I'd seen much of Crescent Galaxy on my own, before meeting Kavita, but after we joined forces, bought Athena, and expanded our reach, I was able to realize just how big this place really was. Some of the farthest-reaching planets had been out of touch for my little bumblebee fighter jet. Oh, the times I had cursed at a bounty that slipped into warp speed and out of my reach...

But not Athena. She'd take us anywhere we wanted to go. As long as she had enough fuel, that is...

"I told them to fill her up, but that's going to drain our credits until we complete this mission," Kavita interrupted my thoughts, grabbing a small rucksack and tossing it over her shoulder. It was empty, but I knew the plan was to fill it with as many supplies as we could afford while we tried to get some intel on the trouble at Tiberius Terminal.

If our mark was there, and these damned spiders were attacking everything, there's a good chance he got trapped there and we wouldn't be able to get to him anytime soon.

"We'll figure something out," I said, following her out the hatch, my feet touching pavement for the first time in nearly a week.

"We always do," she laughed, a low, gravelly laugh that after years together, still made my heart flutter.

We'd been off the ship no more than two minutes before a familiar voice rang out behind us, stopping us in our tracks.

"Dammit," Kavita muttered under her breath.

"Look what the space cats dragged in!" a high-pitched, nasally sounding male voice called through the base. Even over all the hums of engines and equipment, I would recognize him anywhere.

"Bingo," I said coolly, turning to face him. He was another bounty hunter, not as cutthroat as most in our profession, and probably the closest thing to a friend we had amongst our colleagues, but I still wouldn't trust him farther than I could throw him.

As it happens, that wasn't far at all. The portly being was nearly as wide as he was tall. Bingo was a

Billbug, a weevil-like species of organic beings from the outer edge of the galaxy. Their home planet had been destroyed, too, many of them exterminated during the war.

"What are you two sexy ladies doing over here on a shitty little space station like this?" he laughed out his words, and his long snout wobbled in front of his face, his beady eyes squinting together as he rubbed his protruding belly with his right hand.

"Would you believe we were actually looking for you?" I teased dryly.

"Nope. Never!" he bellowed, grabbing at his tummy with the other hand now, that snout just flapping around. "But now that you've found me, wanna hear the latest gossip?"

As a matter of fact, I did. That was one of the only things Bingo was good for. But he could talk the bark off a tree if given the chance. And getting Bingo to tell a story straight way through from start to finish was a task within itself.

Almost as if on cue, Kavita jumped in to help. "We actually really have to get going. Lots to do and we must keep on schedule, of course."

She turned and I fell into step right beside her. "Oh yes, so great to see you Bingo, but we really must be going."

We'd hardly taken more than a couple of steps and he ran on his stubby little legs to keep up with us. "Wait, wait, wait..."

We slowed but didn't stop, and Kavita gave me a sideways look and a wink. The plan was working perfectly.

"Before you go charging in there with your delicate lady senses, let Bingo tell you what's going on out at Tiberus Terminal."

"Go on," I said, lifting one eyebrow. "But do keep up, okay?"

Wiping sweat from his dark brow with one of his four arms, he continued. "Word on the wire is some mecha-spiders were tearing up the joint, ripped the whole damn docking station off, bits of it just floating away into space, along with any people who had the unfortunate luck to be on it, too."

"How terrible for them," Kavita muttered, not stopping, but keeping her pace slow enough the little guy could stick with us.

People were mingling as much as they were moving today, which was typically an unusual thing to see at a space station, but today was no ordinary day. The Red Sun Order had used mecha-bots when they attacked many of our planets. Never ones to get their own hands dirty, the leaders used whatever soldiers they could muster up to do it for them.

The mechas had their own galaxy, off to the left of ours. Ursa Nebula, I believe it was called, and they had never bothered us before the war. But the war changed everything...

"How terrible for *us,* Missy," he corrected, making a *pfffpt* sound as that dangly bit in front of his mouth continued to flop around. "Now, no bounty hunter, space jockey, or interstellar cowboy can get within miles of that shithole and no Tiberius Terminal means -"

"No credits in our coffers," the three of us said in unison. The bug man had a damn point. And I hated him for it.

We stopped walking so abruptly, he bumped into both of our backs, sending my petite frame lurching forward, but Kavita's arm flying out stopped me from propelling face first into the pavement.

"Do you have any real intel, Bingo?" Kavita narrowed her eyes at him. I loved played good cop, bad cop with her when Bingo was concerned. Despite being only three inches taller than me, Kavita had an intimidating way about her that made even the largest of grown men cower when she turned on the glare.

"W-w-w-well... that depends," he stuttered, avoiding eye contact with her. "How much are you paying?"

"That depends entirely -" she leans in close to his beady little eyes and enunciates every single syllable slowly, "On whether or not you have anything worth buying."

"Word is the spiders are scouting the planets for ore," he blurted out, with Kavita inches from his face.

I reach into my pocket and pull out a single bronze-colored coin. We didn't use physical currency anymore since the war, but he could trade this in for at least 100 credits if he was smart about it. Holding the coin in front of his greedy little face, I ask, "What ore?"

He reaches for it, and I pull the coin back with a *tsk tsk*.

"Intel first. Reward after," Kavita reinforces.

"Labradorite," he squeaked, looking around to see if anyone else heard, and reaching again for the coin.

I give it to him with a sigh and he gleefully

presses it to his lips, then slides it into his pocket. "Nice doing business with you, ladies."

"Bugger off," Kavita snaps.

Once he's a few steps away, I ask the burning question on my mind. "What do the spiders want with labradorite?"

"Beat's me," she shrugs. "No one's even seen that mineral since the Milky Way Galaxy was blown up."

"Well, one thing we do know..." I shift the empty water canisters in my hands and look around the space station, "Is mechas don't do anything without a reason."

CHAPTER FIVE

From there, we continued on our mission to get supplies — at least, what we could afford with our meager budget. Water was a hot commodity these days. Not many healthy planets left with fresh water to source from. The space stations all had filtration systems, but water didn't come cheap, especially the kind filtered enough to taste good.

We managed to get two jugs of drinking water and four of other-use water, and Kavita found some affordable food rations and shoved them into her bag.

"This will have to do us until we get that bounty," she grumbled.

"No worries," I assured her, but we had plenty of

reason to worry. We couldn't afford to get much skinnier and if rumors of the attacks were making their way down the radios, vendors would start jacking up the prices of literally everything.

Such was the way of post-war life. If only we could finish this mission and head back to Logara, we could get some reprieve. We had – dare I say it – *friends* – there, and they would take care of us, if need came.

In the years that had passed since that first chance meeting booking Billy the Kid, we'd brought in many a bounty, some that were even more challenging than that first fiasco where we'd both gone for the same mark.

But never had we come across anything like we'd seen earlier. Apparently, we weren't the only ones concerned about it. We made haste of getting our supplies and returning to the ship, not talking much along the way, which gave us opportunity to hear the other conversations buzzing around us.

"Did you hear about Tiberus?"

"They say Red Sun Order is behind it..."

"What do they want with labradorite?"

Most of it was just bits and pieces of the same thing, overlapping voices, plagued with fear and trepidation. But there were a few parts that filled in blanks that Bingo couldn't for us. For one, Tiberius Terminal had been completely destroyed. If our mark was still there, he was either dead, or hiding somewhere trying to remain not-dead.

As badly as we wanted to get to him, we'd be flying Athena straight into a warzone. Rather than risk it, we needed to find out where refugees were going. Our future depending on cashing in this bounty, but I wasn't about to fly into an active battle to get it.

Lucky for us, we'd heard some space jockeys saying that survivors were being ushered out of Tiberus and shuttled to a place call Coreter.

There was so much chaos, they weren't processing ID checks correctly, and there's a good chance our bounty was on one of those shuttles. If we went to Coreter, we might find him.

Right now, it was the best plan we had.

Back on the ship, we put it into autopilot with Memory keeping an eye on things and made our way to the bedroom, if you can even call it a "room".

She could see it in my eyes, no doubt. I'd never

been able to hide my stress from her. I could put on a brave front like the little badass I was for everyone else, but Karina saw right through me. There were times I thought she could see directly into my soul and the very thought terrified me and fascinated me all the same.

No one had ever understood me like she did. And right now, she knew exactly what I needed. The one and only thing that could take my mind off all this stress, the uncertainty, and the madness that we had to face every day was a good, hard orgasm (or two).

As soon as her lips touched mine, my worries melted away.

Her soft, gentle touch sent shivers down my spine, and I responded with a passionate moan. She seemed to know how badly I wanted her as she moved between my legs; every nerve in me begged for more of what only she could provide.

She teased that bundle of nerves that ached for comfort and a distraction from all the stress around us, and all words escaped me - feeling so primal and animalistic under her tender caress.

Then came the sexy whisper: "I want to taste all of you."

Without hesitation I replied, "I'm all yours" –

parting my legs more to give her full access to all of me, wanting nothing more than for this pleasure-filled ride continue even further until we both get our desired satisfaction.

Her touch and her mouth on my throbbing pussy left me wanting more and more as I inched closer toward my eventual orgasm - sending waves upon waves of pleasure through every inch of me until finally, I could hold back no more.

My head flung back onto the pillow, my moans louder now; tangled between what seemed like unending bliss and true passion fulfilled... I couldn't restrain my response. Nor did I want to.

She flicked and sucked and drew me all the way to the edge like no one but her knew how to do. Kavita knew my body as intimately as she knew her own and in times like this, she proved just how much.

My back arched higher as if offering myself even more to her delicious touch — begging for her mercy while wanting all at once never to let go. She held me down at the hips, her fingers pressing into my skin enough to probably cause bruising tomorrow and just when I felt like I could fly right out of my body, she finished me off.

Sucking my clit until I was exploding in her

sweet mouth, she then kissed me back down until my body stopped rocking and I calmed. Sliding up my body, she kissed me all the way back up to my lips, hungrily waiting for her.

"I love you," I whispered.

"I know," she teased. "I love you too, Safari."

CHAPTER
SIX

By morning, I was feeling refreshed, and we were 80% of the way to Coreter. Most of the time, I don't sleep much. It's a combination of stress and trying to maintain a full workday. We had so many things we needed to do before we could achieve our dream of settling down at our new place on Logara.

A house, a lawn, maybe even a little white picket fence. Hell, possibly a couple of kids one day in the future... it was the dream life, and one I never thought possible for a space rat like me, but everything changed after I met Kavita.

Neither of us had started life on Logara. In fact, we came across the little planet by change, while on a job. It was the biggest bounty of our careers, and both of us were hellbent on succeeding.

Harley 'The Sparrow' Swien had been on the top of the Most Wanted charts for years now. He was the golden pearl every bounty hunter dreamed of bagging, but most knew they would never come close.

One day, we got a tip from an informant that he'd been spotted on a small planet inhabited by human survivors of the war. And off we went, in search of the bounty hunter's holy grail. I'm not sure either one of us expected to actually find him, but we were in between jobs and feeling adventurous and restless, so off we went.

Logara was one of the few planets left for human race settlers after the war. Most of the planets that our kind thrived on were completely destroyed. The Red Sun Order killed the inhabitants, mined them for resources, and then blew up what was left so there wasn't even a chance to rebuild.

I'd never been there before, but I had heard about it on my travels. Kavita said she had been once and that it was quiet, but peaceful. Things definitely moved a lot slower on Logara, but I loved that about it. In fact, I found it quite charming. I'd never had a real home – mine had been destroyed when I was barely old enough to remember.

But it seemed like this cozy little planet was just as good as any to make a home. And there was no one else I'd want to do it with than Kavita. For years now, I'd found home in her heart, in the warmth of her embrace, in her soft lips on mine, in the way she could anticipate my every need and desire before I even realized it myself.

It wasn't a difficult decision to take the extra money from our Sparrow bounty and purchase a nice plot of land on Logara. It was just outside the main city limits so we had some peace and quiet on the day-day but could pop on over for city action whenever we wanted.

We'd now been back a few times, tending to the details and meeting the locals. Groundbreaking had already occurred, and our house was set to be complete within the next two months. I'd not been so excited about anything in a long time.

Our plan had been to take on as many bounties as we could over the next two months and save up all the money. Then, when the house was done, we'd take some time off and enjoy it.

Neither of us was ready for retirement yet, but we were both exited about having a little place to call home and being able to steal away for some vacations now and then. This was the closest thing to planning for a future that I'd ever had in life. It was the first time in my whole life I'd dared to dream.

Leaving Coreter, we set out for Strelirus, and hopefully our last stop to find this mark and get this bounty. I was getting angsty about the rumors and really wanted to get back to Logara to check on our property.

And our friends.

But this planet we were headed to was no cakewalk. It was a playground for the top dogs in the galaxy and happened to be the first planet to rebuild after the war.

It had been a long and difficult war. The Red Sun Order hit fast and struck hard, wiping out any planets who had a chance of counterattacking first. They must have been decades – if not more – planning the attacks, building the resources, and plotting how they would carry it out.

They used their mecha-bots to infiltrate planets and dig deep into their core. Then, when no one was suspecting, they detonated and blew them to bits – many full of innocent civilians who all died at the hands of the Red Sun Order.

For the planets who had resources they wanted, they took a different approach. They came in with force, overpowering the people. Those brave enough to fight back were shot down, the rest burned in their homes, or

Afterwards, the universe was in shambles, with hundreds of planets destroyed by the enemy's ruthless attacks.

But there was one planet that managed to make a quick comeback: Strelirus.

Strelirus had been in an ideal position; it was far enough away from the front lines that it escaped much of the destruction, but close enough to the conflict that its resources were invaluable for both sides. As such, Strelirus quickly became a hub for trade and diplomacy during this time of crisis – leading many traders and diplomats from around the galaxy to flock to its shores. The government built strong defenses here and Red Sun Order was never able to infiltrate it directly, or with their mechas. While all the other planets became vast wastelands of destruction, this one remained.

However, what made Strelirus truly unique

wasn't just its strategic location or booming economy – it was also the first planet to rebuild after the war ended. Where others were still struggling with finding food and shelter, Strelirus had already erected skyscrapers, created infrastructure systems and laid out luxurious parks all across their cities.

This allowed them to become a beacon of hope within a broken universe – giving strength to those who lived on other planets as they saw what could be achieved when determination took charge over despair.

The government quickly built refugee houses on the planet and millions who had lost their homes flocked there for a new start, or at the very least, a place to have a roof over their heads until they could begin their new start.

Today, if you look into space at night while flying by, you can see why so many chose Strelirus as their destination: where others are shrouded in darkness due to lack of power or resources, on clear nights you can spot glittering lights coming from every single part of Strelirus.

It's a shining symbol for each person who worked hard towards rebuilding better than before - showing us all that no matter how dark things may seem sometimes we have what it takes rise again even stronger than before.

Despite all that, it had a seedy underbelly, like most big cities. And that's what had led us here on more than one occasion tracking down some wanted criminal so we could pay our own bills. Being a bounty hunter was hard work, but it was honest work, and that was more than I could say for most of the people we picked up in this profession.

CHAPTER SEVEN

As we came in for our landing, I had to take it all in again. I swear this planet had grown even more since the last time we were here, and I didn't think that was possible.

Unlike many of the planets in Crescent Galaxy, Strelirus was built up. Where others were still expanding after the war, Strelirus had expanded to unimaginable heights. The entire planet was one massive city, brightly lit skyscrapers stretching into the skyline, neon signs lighting up the narrow alleyways, and full of sounds no matter what time of day or night you were there.

And the seedy underbelly of Strelirus was where all Crescent Galaxy's Most Wanted went to do their dirty, underhanded business. This wasn't the first time we'd been here and in our line of work, it certainly wouldn't be the last.

We first popped into a place called The Pet Shop, and there were not animals for adoption in here. It was actually a bar and cocktail lounge, and the prime location for kitchen table deals made between some of the Galaxy's worst kind of bad guys.

It was no surprise that our mark was hiding here on Strelirus after narrowly escaping the attack at Tiberius. Our original intel had said he was at the terminal to make a drop off. Now there was a good chance that transaction never took place, with how the spiders were crawling all over the place. We were meeting another contact here at The Pet Shop, and hoping he had some answers for us.

The atmosphere was thick and smoky; it seemed like everyone had something to hide. I could feel the eyes on us as we scanned around for our contact, getting ready to make another deal. We spotted him at a back corner booth tucked away from prying eyes, sipping his drink slowly while he waited for us.

As soon as we reached him, he quickly got down to business without any pleasantries or small talk. It was just as well. Even the walls had ears and eyes in this joint. The less people knew about us and why we were here, the better.

"There's an arms deal going down," he leans in super close as he says the words low. "Between the Black Phantoms and Onyx Snake."

We were familiar with the Black Phantoms and Onyx Snake, two rival gangs who had been looting the galaxy since even before the war. The aftermath of Red Sun Order's destruction just made it easier for them to go undetected. Half our bounties since the war had connections to one of those gangs. It wasn't a total surprise the current mark was involved with them.

But it did mean it might be trickier to get to him.

"Onyx put a blood mark on his head."

"Dammit," Kavita mutters under her breath. A blood mark means Onyx Snake considers him theirs and if we pick him up and turn him in to authorities, we're stepping on *their* toes, too, a fact they will likely not take kindly to.

We left The Pet Shop behind and walked out into the bustling streets of Strelirus - relieved that we were one step closer to completing this mission, despite all odds being against us. I was so in my head, I didn't even see the man in front of me until I slammed right into his chest.

Oof!

"A duel?"

Of course, the bastard wanted to duel us. I'd expect nothing less from one of these characters. I had heard about the strange customs of this planet, but I hadn't expected it would be so soon that I'd have to experience them.

Whenever Kavita and I came here, we tried to keep our heads down, lay low, and get off the planet without anyone recognizing us. Being a bounty hunter was enough to get a target on your back but being a couple of women who put a lot of really, really bad guys away in galactic penitentiary was another thing altogether.

Now this bastard was demanding I duel him because I accidentally bumped into him in a dark alleyway. You can't make this shit up. Nearly brushing him off, I thought better of it. Maybe I could work this to our advantage somehow...

One glance at Kavita showed me she was warning me not to with her facial expressions, but I knew what this planet did to people it saw as weak. And this man was not one I wanted to think I was weak.

He was gruff and menacing, with a wild look in

his eye. He shifted his weight from his left foot to his right as he waited for me to respond.

"This is how we settle matters on Strelirus," he said gruffly. "We fight to prove who's right."

I gulped nervously as I considered my options. Then something inside me stirred - an inner strength that told me not to back down from any challenge. After all, what did I have to lose? If nothing else at least it would make for an interesting story!

So, without further hesitation, I accepted his duel. What choice did I have really?

"Fine. Name the time and place," I finally answer, head held high, determination in my eyes. I'm not one to back down, and that little fact has gotten me into a lot of trouble before. But now...

"At the Park n Ride. Now. In fifteen minutes," he grunted and strutted off.

"Safari..." Kavita warned, but she knew me well enough to know there was no talking me out of this. Letting out a long sigh, she adds, "Just be careful."

The Park n Ride was an old parking garage now turned fight arena. It was illegal, of course, but most things on Strelirus were. We'd picked up a couple of bounties here before in the past and all I could hope for right now is that we wouldn't be recognized or made as bounty hunters. If we were, we'd be dealing with a whole new batch of problems.

Once inside, the doorkeeper seemed to know exactly what I was there for.

Within moments, I was in the arena and staring my opponent in the face. The crowds cheered and jeered, and I could faintly make out Kavita's sweet face and soft lips just behind the cage. They hadn't let her come any further than that, and she held both of our bags as she looked on, steely eyes and poker face.

She knew I could hold my own in a fight. But walking into a battle with no information about your enemy was never the smartest move. I just had to hope luck and experience would be on my side.

The referee did a countdown, and a horn sounded the beginning of the duel. We'd each been patted down for weapons before the start. This show was hands-only.

Taking a deep breath and steeling my nerves, I stepped forward and raised my fists in preparation. We circled each other warily, sizing each other up while searching for an opening. Suddenly he lunged at me, throwing punches wildly at every angle he could find - but luckily, I managed to dodge all of them effortlessly.

CHAPTER SEVEN

Tiny and light on my feet, that was one thing I had going for me. Another was 10 years of martial arts training growing up, many a street brawl as a scrappy teenage vagabond, and more than 10 years of bounty hunting across the galaxy.

He landed a punch to my lower lip and chin, and I felt the warm trickle of blood down my face. I dodged the next two and landed a few to his nose and cheek. He was fast for such a burly man, but not fast enough and not as agile as me. Each punch he missed made the rage on his face grow stronger. He was pissed.

And a pissed man loses logic. This would work in my favor.

The crowd was getting louder and louder, but I couldn't let it distract me. I had to win this stupid testosterone-fueled madness so my woman and I could get back to finding the prick who would ensure our next payday.

My opponent kept attacking relentlessly but none of his strikes made contact; rather than just blocking or parrying his blows away, I used my agility and reflexes to quickly move out of his path instead – almost always leaving him off-balance after his attempt failed miserably once again!

After several minutes of intense back-and-forth

exchanges between us both (not forgetting some truly spectacular dodges on my part), eventually even the toughest spectator began cheering louder than ever before as they realized who would be emerging victorious tonight: Me.

I walked away from the duel with a bloody lip and my pride intact.

Kavita walked away counting fistfuls of old-school paper money. We'd have to trade it in for current credits somewhere, but it was still an impressive haul.

"Did you bet on my duel?" I asked incredulously.

"Of course, I did." She said it with such a straight face that all I could do was stand there and grin.

That's my girl…

CHAPTER
EIGHT

There was one more good thing to come out of my duel. The event had dragged our bounty out of hiding. Memory spotted him first; his calculative brain and impeccable data storage spotted his face in the crowd. Then Zion helped tail him after it was over. They followed him back to where he had been staying, Zion hot on his scent. And this afforded us an amazing opportunity to make our capture and get off this lawless planet before anymore impromptu duels.

They had him inside an old shed in the back alley of a strip mall, keeping eyes on him until we arrived. It seemed to be where he was calling home these days, and he was in there alone. Not only would he have no idea we were coming, but he'd have no time to prepare a counterattack. This is what we needed.

Get in. Get the mark. Get out.

Nice and clean. That's how we liked to do our jobs.

We arrived on foot, careful not to make any noise. Memory had turned off all his lights and was keeping extra quiet. Zion is an excellent hunter and stalks his prey like a thief in the night, so there was no way he was detected as he waited for us.

Once we arrived on location, Kavita sent Memory back to get the ship ready. We'd need to get our mark back and locked into the ship's brig, with our electronic cuffs on him, and get out of here quickly before anyone caught us.

I was all for a little razzle dazzle when needed, but on Strelirus, a planet built by misfits and thieves, it made more sense to be as quiet as possible on this arrest and extraction. We already had a positive ID from Memory so all we really had to do was nab the guy.

Looking through one broken, dusty window into the shed, he was sitting on a fold-out sofa bed, counting packets of a powdery substance that most definitely wasn't legal. I had no clue if his door was locked, but we were about to find out.

Nodding to me with the go-ahead, Kavita moved toward the little wooden door that looked barely enough to keep the elements out. In one fluid movement, she kicked the door in with her favorite knee-high black boots. I was through the threshold before he could get all the way up from his seat.

Not hesitating for even a second with my ray gun, I fired an electronic bolt straight into his midsection that would knock him out for a few minutes to a couple of hours at best, but wouldn't cause any lasting harm, apart from a small bruise, at worst.

His body slumped to the floor, hitting the coffee table on the way down and Kavita was on him in a heartbeat, slapping the cuffs on his limp wrists.

"Good job, babe."

We tossed his ragdoll body over Zion's back and began walking back toward our ship. No lights. If anyone saw us right now, there'd be hell to pay, for sure. But this was a planet full of outlaws and one good thing about that: people mind their own damn business.

We had him on the ship and locked in within the

half hour and then we were ready to take back to the skies, but we needed one more thing first.

Before we left, we stopped in a little corner shop that sold weapons, explosives, and treats you hardly found anymore since the war. Candy bars, tampons, and even a tube of mascara now and then. Kavita hit the goldmine once when she found a hair straightener and a curling wand in some old hole-in-the-wall shop on a small planet at the edge of the galaxy. I was most certainly *not* a wash-and-go type of gal.

These are the things nobody thinks about when the actual apocalypse hits them. I walked around half blind for three months before I found a shady street vendor who had some glasses almost in my prescription. I had to trade my very best pistol and my last slice of bread to get them but what the hell was I going to do with a gun when I was blind as a bat?

Thankfully, since then, some planets had gotten back to enough normalcy, and I earned enough through my bounty hunting to get a laser surgery done. Before the war, I had worn contacts. But not even *I* was brave enough to put post-apocalyptic contacts into my own eyeballs. Who the hell knows what would happen?

"Hey look," Kavita said, holding up a little packet of candy. "Fizz-its!"

It was her favorite candy and we hardly ever seen it since shit hit the fan out here. They were tiny hard candies that fizzled and popped in your mouth.

"Get two, my love." Smiling across the aisle, I grabbed a battery-powered flashlight and a jug of drinking water. Who was I to deny my lady the little pleasures in life? She had more than earned it putting up with me for all this time.

As we left the store, I took note of an old security camera in the corner and nodded at Memory. He knew the drill and immediately worked to short-circuit the camera feed.

Get in. Get out. Undetected.

It's how we had gotten by for so long so far. We couldn't risk leaving any footprint behind, especially on this planet.

With our mark securely safely in the ship's brig, we charted our course to Sohiter, where Mr. Lovelace would be eagerly awaiting us. He'd been after this sack of shit for a long time, so long he even added a 50,000-credit bonus for the first person to bring him in.

Once we were in the air and safely on autopilot, we stepped away from the cockpit and into the bedroom we had built for ourselves on Athena. Slightly bigger than my old Bumblebee, we had room for the brig in the back, a supply closet, arms area, and our own bedroom, which Kavita had helped me decorate to our tastes.

When we were in here, it was easy to forget out the rest of the galaxy, the war, the pain that so many had endured, the bad guys we chased down on a regular basis – all of it. In here, we were in our safe space. And my favorite part of our safe space was making love to Kavita.

Not 60 seconds had passed before she was on me, kissing me, stroking my body, tangling her fist in my hair, and tasting me like it was the first time every time.

One thing I loved about kissing Kavita: she never held back. Like most things in her life, when she did something, she did it 100% percent. Every kiss was like the first taste of her all over again and I felt myself melting into her until you could no longer tell where I stopped, and she began.

Her kiss was a challenge I was all too happy to

meet. Pressed against the wall, she pushed her tongue in my throat, eliciting a slight happy moan from me. From there, she slid her hands up and down my body, caressing me, squeezing me, and urging me melt under her touch.

Like a sorceress, using her touch and kisses to cast spells of pleasure all over my body, she unwound me, and I loved it. I felt the warmth rising inside me as she tenderly explored my left breast through my shirt with her proficient fingers while our tongues roamed in unison through each other's mouths making us gasp for air.

Kavita tugged at my top, desperate to free my budding nipples from the confines of this shirt. She'd wiggled one out and was rolling it between her fingers as I rocked my hips into her. She kissed me passionately and my body trembled at her touch - every nerve alive from head to toe.

I needed her. It had been too long. She shoved her right leg in between mine, her thigh going right where I needed it most and I couldn't stop myself from grinding against her, my arms wrapped rightly around her back.

My heart raced in anticipation at what more could come but then it stopped when I heard those blissful words spoken into delicate ear, "I want to taste you."

"Mmmm, yes please!" It's all I can manage to get out before she's tossing me onto our bed and leaning over top of me. She pulls my shirt over my head now, exposing my rock-hard nipples and begins kissing her way down my neck, my chest, and to my breasts – first the left and then the right.

Our bodies were intertwined in an electric embrace, as my senses filled with the sweet aroma of her perfume.

Her delicate lips sent flames of pleasure coursing through my veins as she licked and sucked at my rock-hard nipples. But I knew she would only settle here for a moment.

I felt her gentle breath tickle against the sensitive skin of my chest before feeling a blissful sensation overtake me, leading to an enveloping warmth that started from head and slowly moved all the way down until it reached between my legs.

She kissed and licked and nibbled me all the way down to the soft, hot, burning wetness between my thighs, and as she buried her head between them, I grabbed her head with my hands, my fingers tangling in her dark hair.

Gods, she was sexy!

And never sexier than when she had her head between my legs. Kavita loved eating pussy, and there was nothing in this galaxy I loved more than getting eaten out. It was one of many reasons we worked so well.

I spread my legs wide, giving her better access as she goes to town on my cunt as if she is starving.

With each flick or bite came utter delight until finally I tilted back and let out a moan so loud it echoed off the walls around us - no longer able to contain this ecstasy flooding over me while this woman worked some kind unheard magic.

The mark probably heard me if he was awake, but I couldn't be bothered to care as I came apart in her arms, my come on her lips.

CHAPTER NINE

After our romp in the bedroom, we had to head back to the cockpit and make sure this ship was still headed in the right direction. I trusted Athena to manage autopilot when we were just coasting but a machine was still a machine, and only as good as the sentient being who programs it.

I knew it would need to be a quickie, especially with a bounty on board. We never liked to leave them unsupervised for long, in the brig or not. And although we had Zion and Memory to let us know if anything went sideways, I could never let my guard down enough to completely surrender (to making love or to sleep) when we had someone else on board.

CHAPTER NINE

The sooner we dropped this bastard off and collected the reward, the better. I wanted to fuck my lady good and hard all night long, then sleep all the next day, our exhausted naked bodies entwined in the sheets and one another.

That's why after we each chased one delicious orgasm a piece, we put our clothes back on and headed back to the front of the ship. Memory had been hard at work gathering data for us.

It included details of our trajectory, the current mission, our dwindling fuel levels, and all the information he could hack across the airwaves regarding the attacks on Tiberus. Apparently, attacks had happened at other planets and space stations as well, all over the past couple of days.

The data dump was mind-boggling, and I had to blink a few times just to clear my senses before I could process it. Kavita leaned over my shoulder, looking at the same reports.

"This is madness," she muttered.

"I really hope this isn't the beginning of another war," I started, but she shushes me with a finger to my lips. She didn't like talking about the war and hated talking about future war even more. I understood. We'd all been through hell, but Kavita had experienced the worst that war can bring.

"We have to stop at Hope for refueling," she said and Memory beep-beeped in agreeance behind her. I don't even feel angry at her for changing the subject. It's just as well. No need to start worrying about things that haven't happened yet. I should know this better than anyone.

Even so, I wasn't crazy about needing to stop at Hope. I was hoping we'd make it a straight shot back to complete our mission and collect our bounty, but we were too far out. We couldn't fly there on good intentions, unfortunately, so a stop would be mandatory.

I had nothing against the space satellite Hope, but I wasn't keen on stopping with one of the Galaxy's Top 10 Most Wanted in our brig. It only takes a moment for something bad to happen.

"That's fine, but only one of us can leave the ship. I don't trust him."

"Of course," she agreed, nodding toward the brig at the back of our ship. It was reinforced with physical and electronic barriers. We had chains and bars, and digital locks that were tied into the ship's controls.

Not to mention there was the electric fence gate over the doorway, and there were the electric cuffs we had on him. These couldn't be broken by any object in the solar system. But again, nothing was foolproof. I'd learned that the hard way enough times to know not to take chances.

So, that meant when we stopped at Hope Station to refuel, one of us would be staying with the mark, guns trained on him, and not taking any chances. If he so much as farted wrong, he'd lose his head.

As we pulled into the docking station at Hope Satellite, Kavita decided I should be the one to hop off and handle business.

"You are due to stretch your legs," she smiled, kissing me on the forehead. I didn't argue. A ten-minute walk around the satellite wouldn't hurt anything. In fact, it sounded like just what I needed.

As the jockeys refueled our ship, I went to pay, scanning my card to debit the credits. The thought crossed my mind to check for snacks for Kavita in here, but then I remembered they have little in the way of extras on Hope.

Everything about satellite life boiled down to two things: conservation of resources and not getting sucked away into space. Life – if you could call it that – was fast-paced here. No one intentionally lived on a satellite. They were built and carefully located in between growing planets within the system that were being rebuilt since the war.

Think of them as little space pit stops. Fuel up your ship, get supplies for yourself, and be on your merry little way. Of course, people had to man these stations, and most of them did live here, but only for a few weeks to a few months at a time. Then, they traded shifts and went back home to their families, and new workers came in to take their place.

Any time I'd ever visited a satellite, I found the people difficult to connect with but the way they operated wildly fascinating. Everything has a place. Everyone has a purpose. Like a finely tuned rig, it must operate according to plan, lest it just float away into the abyss of space and time itself.

Today, the energy felt different. I couldn't put my finger on it, but something felt off, and I longed to be back on Athena with Kavita almost as soon as my feet touched the metal ground at Hope platform.

"Fill it up please," I said to the jock at the fueling station, and then I went over to the computer to pay. As I scanned in my card, it flashed a "Low Credits" warning and showed me our meager balance.

"Yeah, yeah, I know," I muttered to the machine, but mostly to myself. We had the richest bounty we'd ever picked up in our careers sitting right there in the back of Athena. We just needed enough fuel to get his sorry as back so we could collect. Everything was quite literally riding on this bounty.

Living payday to payday was hard, but things were especially tight since we sank all our savings into the land and starting our build on Logara. But it was worth it. It was worth every penny when I thought about my future with Kavita. We were building something tougher; something neither of us ever had growing up, and that meant more than a billion credits to me.

Just then another ship docked at Hope's fueling station and two bearded men hopped out. They wore insignia I couldn't recognize, and they walked like no one else in the world mattered. The taller one shoulder-checked me as they passed by.

"Hey, watch it!" I shouted, but I'm not sure he even noticed he had hit me. *Fucking men.* As I turned back to what I was doing, I couldn't help but overhear part of their conversation.

"Yeah, they blew the whole damn thing to smithereens. Can you imagine?"

The one on the right shook his head ruefully. "Who would do such a thing? And why?"

"Pffft!" the other one scoffed. "You know who."

"But the Red Sun Order was eradicated. You know that. We were there, Jim."

"Yes, I was," he muttered, shaking his head. "And that's how I know we didn't destroy them. We only slowed them down."

What? I thought to myself. Was it possible that the Red Sun Order wasn't really killed off? That a threat could still be out there and now they were attacking again? It made no sense!

But then again, it made all kinds of sense. The "powers that be" wanted so badly to begin rebuilding the galaxy, they would say anything to make the people feel at-ease. And they would do anything to get elected and remain in power, even if that meant lying to the very people they were supposed to be protecting.

Politics... some things never change.

I finished up the transactions quickly and raced back to the ship. I needed to tell Kavita what I had overheard.

CHAPTER TEN

Climbing back onto the ship, sighing heavily, I couldn't hide my concern as I told Kavita, "Let's get out of here, now." I plop down in my co-pilot seat and strap myself in. Kavita was an excellent pilot, but the launch of off Hope was always a bit rocky due to its location near a big asteroid field.

Zion perked up from where he was resting on the floor, one ear tipped up and the other flopped over. I nod at him but say nothing. He gives me a long, hard look up and down and then lays his head back down.

"Something wrong?" She asks, knowing full well she can read me like an open book. She also knows that I will rarely speak up without being asked if something is bothering me. The words those captains had said were still ringing loudly in my ears.

"Shit's going down out there," I nod toward the vastness of space in front of us. "I mean, even more than usual. But I'd rather talk about it more when we get this shitstain off our ship."

I say that last part a bit louder, not caring if the mark can hear me. He was a true bastard, wanted for eight counts of murder, three of them children. I'd kill him myself were it not for the fact that the victims' families deserved the proper trial and sentencing. I wouldn't rob them of their closure.

Usually, I didn't get emotional about the missions. This was just a job and the best way to do it efficiently and successfully was not to get emotionally invested. But this guy was the lowest of the low and it was hard not to have feelings about him and what he did.

Thankfully, we were only a few more hours away from Sohiter. Athena would make it in hyperdrive, and it'd only take two, but that drained a lot of fuel, which wasn't something we could afford right now. Once we claimed this bounty, then maybe I could sing a different tune.

We arrived at Sohiter and docked in the

incoming bays. There were a couple of other ships there already, but none that I recognized. It was just as well. We had a strong reputation in the industry and as a result, some of the other bounty hunters didn't take too kindly to us.

For the misogynists, the only thing worse than a woman doing a "man's job", was when she did it even better than him. It probably wouldn't earn us any brownie points with them to come walking in with a bag like this in our cuffs.

Of course, they'd find out eventually. News of a capture like this would spread like wildfire. But the gossip and rumor mill wasn't my concern. Getting this bastard inside and secured with Mr. Lovelace was my only concern right now.

"I'll get him, and you get my back?" Kavita lays out the plan and I agree. "Secure the doors behind us," she says to Memory. That robot dog was the smartest and most loyal companion I'd ever know besides my own Zion.

I'd known Kavita for two years before she ever told me the full story of how she got Memory. She had grown up in the Alpha Orion quarter. Her mother and father were lower class, working two jobs most of her life just to keep some bread on the table.

She got her love of tinkering by hanging out at the old space junkyard near her house. Most of it was filled with scrap metal, broken machinery and forgotten memories from a bygone age. But for one young girl, it held something much more special: a ticket to an unknown future.

Kavita didn't know what she wanted to be when she grew up. She just knew she didn't want to be like her parents, working their fingers to the bone for no thanks and a meager pay that barely kept the lights on.

She loved spending her days in the dusty old junkyard looking for treasures among all the discarded detritus. She often found interesting gadgets and gizmos that she could use to create new inventions or repair broken ones. This is how she first discovered she could reprogram the old electronics and robotics. Some of the tech was decades old, but she had a natural knack for it.

Some of the things she rebuilt or invented herself from the scraps she found in the junkyard, she sold at a dusty old flea market in town. Kavita was just 12 years old when she first started riding her old mecha-bike into the small town to offer her wares. It supplemented the meager income her parents made, and it gave her great pride to be able to do it.

One day, when Kavita was rummaging through an ancient pile of parts, she found something remarkable: A large robotic dog made out of scraps and wires!

She dusted him off and turned him on, but of course, nothing happened. He was also missing a leg and his ears were broken. But she was smitten with the white machine.

Doing what she does best, Kavita took him home and fiddled with him until she got him to power back up again, his red eyes zooming to life and making direct contact with her big, brown, inquisitive eyes. She knew right away that this robot pup would be her closest companion - so she named him Memory.

At first Memory seemed like any other pet; he played fetch with Kavita in the junkyard and kept her company while she tinkered with machines. But as time went on, Memory began displaying qualities unlike other machines she had built – he responded to commands like a well-trained guard dog but also showed signs of true intelligence too!

It didn't take long for her to realize that Memory

wasn't just another pet; he had the capacity to learn. She fed him all the information and data she could find, and he ate it up, growing more intelligent with each new piece she provided him with. Soon, they scoured the junkyard together looking for data cards and old hard drives he could use to expand his knowledge base. And when Kavita lost her parents and ultimately left her planet, she took him with her.

With his help they explored distant galaxies together, solved mysteries both big and small, created incredible inventions, and eventually became a bounty hunter team, much like me and Zion.

In no time at all he became one of Kavita's most treasured possessions and closest friends– not just because he could do things no ordinary animal could do but because his presence always reminded her about how far you can go if you never give up on your dreams...no matter where you find them.

And since then, the dog had never left her side. He was also the only piece of her home she still had.

———

CHAPTER TEN

Lugging in this bounty, waiting to collect our reward, we overheard the news about Logara. Kavita was the first to hear our planet's name mentioned on the mouths of some vagabonds who were in cuffs awaiting booking.

"They said Logara was attacked," she whispered to me without turning her head in my direction.

"What the hell do those buffoons know about Logara?"

"One of 'em says he's from there or something. Says the whole place was taken over by mecha bugs, infiltrated late last night."

"What the hell?" I mutter under my breath but stop short of my next question when a tall, burly man with three eyes steps in front of us.

"Good job, as always, ladies," Mr. Lovelace purrs, holding out a digital device. I pull our data card from my pocket and plug it into the machine. With a few presses of the buttons, he transfers the 250,000 credits to our account.

I almost want to cry in relief when I see the numbers tick up in our balance, but I maintain a straight face. Holding my emptions in was something I'd become a pro at after my childhood.

"Always a pleasure, Mr. Lovelace," I say. Kavita

nods, and he looks her way only for a moment before turning on his heels and clacking away. Nothing about Mr. Lovelace was a pleasure, but that was neither here nor there.

"Until next time..." he calls from down the hallway.

Shoving the data card back into my pocket, I turn to my girlfriend. We were both certain there would be a next time. 250,000 credits don't last nearly as long as they used to, but at least for now, we have some security. And nothing felt more important to me than finding out what was happening on Logara, and how we could help.

"Let's go home," we say at the same time. *Or whatever home we had left after this attack...*

CHAPTER
ELEVEN

The whole ride back to Logara, Memory was data mining for any news reports that might give us more details on what was happening. It seemed any planet the mechas attacked went radio silent, making it even more difficult to know what was happening. People were talking over comms, some of them in code, but who could be certain they were a reliable source? No, the only way to know for sure was to see it with our own eyes.

We jumped into action and flew through space towards Logara as fast as our ship could take us, flipping on warp speed for at least half of the trip. Athena was fast, but it had never felt it took so long to get home before.

As we approached, it was apparent that we would not be able to just fly in and land at the docking station. It was going to take some fancy piloting to get us in undetected. Luckily, my baby was the best pilot in the galaxy.

Kavita pulled her in for a rough landing, skidding across the surface of the planet in a green field that only slightly cushioned the landing, and we would most assuredly need to do some repairs before we flew out again. But we were here, and that's what matters right now.

The docking station had been destroyed, just like at Tiberus, but we had to get down there and help, one way or another.

The same mechanical spiders we had seen on Tiberus Terminal were crawling all around us. We'd seen then scurrying across the surface before we made our landing, but it looked even worse from here on the ground.

It seemed they were programmed to destroy incoming landings first, so the docking station, flight buildings and basically the entire airport area were a total loss. Fires burned and deep black smoke rolled up from it all, burning our throats to breathe in.

CHAPTER ELEVEN

The spiders were everywhere and wreaking havoc on the planet's surface. "Let's go," Kavita says, grabbing extra ammo and tossing it over her back in one graceful, fluid movement. Even in times of war, she was a majestic creature.

We don't hesitate for a second - immediately jumping out of the ship with guns blazing at the mechanical spiders. Turns out, they shoot back.

As bullets whizzed around us, Kavita expertly maneuvered her way around enemy fire while I ducked behind her for protection before shooting off rounds myself. Regular bullets wouldn't do anything against mechas, but we had loaded our special ammo. It pierces their bullet-proof armor with tiny little legs, then it injects a material that breaks down the metals they are made from.

In addition, Kavita had a special ray-gun that shoots electricity at a voltage that deep-fries their circuit breakers. One pop from that baby and... no more mecha-spider. They just fall over, legs up in the air, out of commission. Unfortunately, we only have one of these guns, so I still need to provide extra cover for her while she takes out as many as she can with it.

Bullets from the spiders are whizzing past our

heads as we approach, and I quickly see there are some locals trying to fight back as well. A shop owner leads a charge of people with handmade torches, lighting the spiders on fire.

This method works a bit slower but achieves the same end goal. If their circuit boards are burned, they shut down. Smart thinking on their parts.

Kavita and I worked together like a well-oiled machine; each of us taking down multiple spiders at once with precision accuracy until eventually none remained standing. Sweat's pouring off my face and neck, the smoke makes it difficult to breathe and my lungs cough and sputter in protest, but we've got them.

For now.

"Good job," my voice is hoarse, and barely above a whisper. Kavita just pats my ass in reply and reaches for a water bottle attached to her rucksack. She passes it to me, and I take a big swig, looking out over the destruction and the people of Logara who are huddled together, women and children crying.

One familiar face stands out in the crowd. She's dirty, soot-stains on her face, but I could know her anywhere. She's the first real friend we made on this planet. Passing the water bottle back to Kavita, I head over to our friend, with my girl right behind me.

"Persephone, what happened here?" I wiped the tears from her cheeks and gave her a moment to compose herself before answering.

"It was just a normal day," she explained through her sobs. "I was outside working in the garden when I heard a strange noise coming through the sound barrier. Looking up, there was a fiery streak across the sky."

She stopped, hiccupping a bit, and a I gently stroked her back as she composed herself.

"Take your time," Kavita whispered, kneeling down on the other side of her.

"There was a crashing sound, echoed across the whole way, and then the sirens started to sound at the docking station. The fire department deployed, and I heard lots of yelling. A group ran by me on foot, armed with guns, and yelled at me to get inside my house."

Putting the pieces together as she told her version of the story, the anger was swelling in my chest. This was our home and our people, and I wouldn't stand for having them attacked like this. One look at Kavita's face said she was feeling the same thing.

"I did what they said and from inside, I called my mom. She said that dad said something had attacked the docking station and they all went out to defend it. I stayed on the line with her until something broke our connection. The next thing I knew, those spider things were running around outside my house, shooting at everything."

She was crying harder now, and I didn't want to push her talk about it anymore.

"Shh, it's okay," I said, wrapping my arm around her. "You're safe now. Can you stand?"

She nodded, and I helped her to her wobbly feet. Not wanting to ask her about the state of her home, due to how upset she already was, we helped her over to the fire department where they had set up temporary shelter and medical aid. We didn't know much more than that yet, but we'd figure it out and help our friends.

At this point, I didn't even know if our partially built house was still standing. Thinking about it sent waves of unease through my stomach. But one thing at a time. We were meeting a friend at a nearby restaurant to discuss what had happened here. He was on the Fire Brigade, and they were first responders, so he knew as much as anyone would about the attack.

CHAPTER ELEVEN

Saying goodbye to Persephone and promising to come back to check on her, we headed over to the Gosco Grill. Despite some damage to the parking lot and the roof, it was still standing and looked in pretty good shape.

CHAPTER TWELVE

We had arrived early, and looked a hot mess after fighting outside, but any other patrons who milled about looked the same. Along with shellshocked looks on their faces, most of them were sipping coffee, crying, or leaning against their loved ones. It seemed like this place has also turned into a bit of a shelter for survivors.

Any still-standing building would likely need to become multipurpose until we could clean up and rebuild. I didn't see Reece here yet, so we had some time before our meeting.

"Safari, come here." She motioned to me from the bathrooms, and I followed her in, the door slamming behind us. There was no lock, but there were three different bathroom stalls in here. Considering the war waging outside, it also looked spotless clean in here.

Logarians always took great care of their spaces and their belongings. It was one thing we loved about this planet – their respect for everything and everyone was admirable.

She washed her hands in the sink with a nice-smelling soap and I followed suit, also splashing some water on my face and neck. After washing her own, she grinned a mischievous little smile and walked toward the stalls.

"Follow me," she crooked her finger at me, beckoning me to her.

Sliding into the stall on the farthest end of the bathroom, she dropped her rucksack on the floor, motioning for me to come in with her. I didn't need to be told twice. Kavita could command my attention like no one else, and I was more than happy to submit.

She knew what I needed, even when I didn't fully.

Following her into the bathroom stall, I dropped my pack, too, and she pulled me in close for a long kiss. Her hand behind my neck was soothing, her tongue in my mouth safe and familiar. This is what I needed – just me and her forever.

No matter what happened on our missions, what we had both experienced in our pasts, the war, or anything the future could bring, one thing that remained constant and kept me grounded was my time with her.

We had to steal our precious moments whenever we could. And we did...

With her lips on mine, I forget about the spiders. Hell, I forget we're in a bathroom stall, the fresh smell of pine and chemicals filling my nostrils. All I can think about is her, her touch, her lips on mine...

Moaning into her mouth, my hands ran through her tangled hair, and down her back, to the lower part of her back, pulling her into me, wishing I could just melt into her and forget everything that we had just gone through.

I hardly even noticed her unbuttoning my pants as her tongue danced with mine behind our lips.

After a few moments, she pulled her lips away, sliding down my body with her hands and pulling my pants down to my ankles in one hard yank. I gasped and giggled, my body heating up with anticipation. She cupped my pussy with her hand and could feel my heat immediately.

CHAPTER TWELVE

"You're already wet," she whispered. "Good girl."

Damn, she knew what those words did to me. If I was wet before, I was positively dripping now.

"I need your pussy, Safari," she demanded, but I was already making the way for her.

Kicking one leg out of my pants, I propped it up on the toilet seat, making room for her to move underneath. She dropped her jacket to the floor before falling to her knees, worshipping me like it was the first time, although we'd done this thousands of times over by now.

She wasted no time burying her head between my spread legs, parting my lips with her tongue, and licking long and slow up my center. I couldn't stifle my moan, which echoed through the empty bathroom.

My hands held tightly to her hair and head as she found my swollen clit and worked it between her lips and tongue, licking and flicking me nearly to the edge. We had to make this quick, given the time and place, but she knew a good tongue-fucking could relax me like nothing else and the thrill of doing it here in a public place always heightened the sensation for me.

Within seconds I was bucking and writhing and

with one hand in her hair and one bracing myself against the walls of the bathroom stall, I felt like I was coming apart at the seams. She held one strong arm around my waist, the other at my thigh as she tongued me deeper. I moved my hips in rhythm to her thrusts, fucking her face with an urgency that even surprised me a bit.

"Fuck, gonna come!" I groan as she flicks my clit those last few times, bringing me over the edge.

I bite my hand to keep from crying out too loud, and cum so hard, my juices run out of her mouth. She takes down all that she can, kissing and licking me clean, swallowing all of me before rising from the floor to kiss me on the lips, my taste still all over her sweet mouth.

Goddess knows I wanted nothing more than to return the favor right now, but she told me to wait. "Later," she grinned. She always was more patient than me.

"Okay later," I squeezed her pussy through her pants. "This is mine."

"As you wish," she giggled and began grabbing her things from the floor of the stall.

Washing our hands in the sink, and looking in the bathroom mirrors, I realized what a mess I was in. My white-blond hair, cut short to shoulder-length, was frizzed out and stained with dirt and grease.

"Going to need a long, hot shower after this," I laughed.

"You and me both," she said, scrubbing dirt from her face with wet paper towels over the sink.

We just needed to get presentable, and have our meeting with Reece, then we planned to go by our property and check on the state of things. Regardless of how it looked, we'd need to stay in a hotel tonight because our house wasn't completed anyway. There was no electricity or running water or anything else set up yet.

This time when we left the bathroom, a friendly face greeted us from a few feet away, already set up in a booth. Waving back, we made our way over to Reece who planned to debrief us on what had happened before we arrived here.

CHAPTER THIRTEEN

"We were just getting cleaned up a bit," Kavita said as we dropped our packs and slid into the booth across from him.

I try to stop the blush spreading across my cheeks, but I doubt he notices anyway. He's wringing his hands over a cup of still-steaming coffee.

"No doubt I need the same," Reece chuckled before getting down to business. "Good job out there, ladies."

"It was nothing," Kavita replied, and I knew she meant it literally. We were both upset we got here too late to do more than clean up the remaining mechas.

As if he could tell what we were both thinking, he continued. "We need you. And this isn't over. Word has it, the mecha were sent here to farm our planet for ore."

"Labradorite," I say, and my voice comes out dry. It's not quite a statement and not quite a question.

"You heard?" He asks, raising an eyebrow.

"Not from a reliable source, but rumor, yes," Kavita confirms.

"It would seem they need this ore and they're targeting every planet known to have it. Rather than negotiate with us, or see if we're willing to sell or trade, they are just taking what they want, at all costs."

"So, we've seen," Kavita muttered under her breath.

"Do we know who sent them?" I asked, fearful of the answer.

"Not for certain," he sighs loud and long, taking a sip from his mug of steaming coffee without even blowing on it first. "Of course, everyone fears the Red Sun Order, but we can't jump to any conclusions. As you know, the government said they had been completely wiped out."

"But who can trust the government these days?"

I blurted. My thoughts went back to that conversation I had heard.

"Exactly." He nodded, looking around as if someone would hear and report us, but the only people in here were too caught up in their own shock and grief to notice us, much less hear what we were saying. "Word is, some of them have been holed up on Planet 281, regrouping, rebuilding, and waiting for the chance to attack again."

Kavita and I had heard that same rumor. Planet 281 was a cold, dark, tiny planet in the farthest point of our galaxy; nearly in the next one over. I'd never been there but another bounty hunter had once brought a fugitive in who had been hiding out there for months. His skin was pale white, all the color drained, his eyes a very light blue, and he was suffering from hypothermia when they brought him in unconscious.

All the bounty hunter chats were blowing up about it – no one had ever brought someone in from that far out in the galaxy before. It wasn't known if he was even going to live, but miraculously, he pulled through. I'm not sure he was as grateful for that now that he's serving four consecutive life sentences on a maximum-security prison planet, but that's another story.

"Can a humanoid race even survive on 281?" She asked what I was thinking.

"Typically, no, but they have mecha support."

Reece made a good point. With the machines they had, they could likely manipulate the environment to sustain a comfortable living on any planet they chose.

"But, if it's not Red Sun, then who?" I didn't realize I had said it out loud until they both looked my way.

"There are rumors about that, too," he says, sipping from his mug. "But none of them very solid. I... I just don't know."

Kavita shifted in her seat, "I don't give a damn who's behind it; we're going to stop them."

"In the meantime, we need to protect the planet. As long as there is labradorite here, the spiders will keep returning in droves." I'd never seen our friend look so weathered and weary; not that I have any questions regarding why.

"What's the plan?" Kavita asks, leaning on her elbows on the table. Instinctively, I run a hand along her back to comfort her.

"We have some shields ready to deploy above the atmosphere. It will block outgoing ships, so we'll need someone to man that, and any outgoing vessels need to get a clearance first. But it will also stop anything from landing here, too. We're going to need some extra hands to get it all up and running in short order, but we estimate we can complete that by end of day tomorrow if we start at sunup."

"We'll be there," we said in unison. I'll never tire of how we do that, completely unplanned. I've never been so in tune with anyone in my life unless you count Zion. And he's a wolf.

"Sounds good." She adds, looking around the restaurant as if taking in our surroundings fully for the first time.

"From there, we need to build an army of defenders. Being that Logara is a peaceful planet, we have only volunteers to work with."

"And you have us," I agree, and Kavita nods.

"That's what I was counting on," he grins, but it's a weary smile, the worry and fatigue betraying him through his eyes.

"We'll be there in the morning. Thanks for your help, Reece."

"Believe me, we should be thanking *you*," he says as he stands, shaking our hand and patting us each on the back.

He walks out of Gosco, but my stomach growling loudly is a sure reminder that we've not eaten since yesterday, and neither of us has had a properly cooked meal in two weeks, since we began our last mission.

At least now we could afford one.

"Let's stay and eat," Kavita hands me a menu even though we both know it by heart from all the times we've been to Gosco's. "Then we'll go find a room."

Not having had a cooked meal in ages, we would have cleared our plates regardless, but Gosco's did a great job, as usual. The sweet little server told us the manager had declared it "on the house", but we still tipped the bill.

The people of this planet needed all the help they could get, especially now.

Leaving the restaurant, we grabbed some rental scooters from the town to get to our land faster than walking. It was about three miles out from the restaurant, and while we had a land vehicle in our ship, Athena was busted and we hadn't been back here in a while anyway, so watching the two suns set on the horizon would be a nice treat.

This truly was a beautiful planet. More than worth fighting for.

"There she is," Kavita cooed as we rolled up on our property, our shell of a house sat untouched on a small hill. It was a two-story modern design with full glass walls in the back, where it overlooked a large lawn and a beautiful view of the sunset.

Our plot of land was far enough outside the city that it had been untouched by the spiders, thankfully. Our house was still intact, and it didn't appear they'd ever made their way out here – yet.

Just to be certain, we went inside and cleared all the rooms. It wasn't a mansion, but it was a fairly large house.

"Let's save room to grow into it," Kavita had said with a wink that day we finalized the building plans.

We had four bedrooms, four and a half bathrooms, a home gym, a practice range, and many other small custom details that were perfect for us. We wanted a large soaking tub in the main bath and a walk-in shower that fit both of us. There was an eat-in kitchen and a huge dining room – far more than just the two of us would ever need. But the hope was that we would have people to invite over one day, found family to share holidays with, and all that.

CHAPTER THIRTEEN

"I guess we better head back," I say, wrapping my arms around her from behind. She strokes my hands with her own, then clasps her fingers through mine.

"Yep, early start tomorrow."

As relieved as I was that the spiders hadn't ruined our home, this wasn't the end and she and I both knew it.

As Reece said, they would return. If they wanted ore that our planet housed in its mountains or core, they would not stop coming until they got it. And although we were all a bit still on edge in the aftermath of the war, it was hard to think the Red Sun Order didn't have something to do with this.

They were descendants of earth, many generations removed. And they had long been trying to rebuild an Earth-like planet. Supposedly, that's what started the war. They felt entitled to all the resources in the galaxy if they suited their needs. I suppose it wasn't enough that their ancestors destroyed their own home planet; they had to destroy all of ours in search of a New Earth. That was pretty much all I knew about it, and even most of that came from the rumor mill.

Earth had been destroyed centuries before I was born. The humans who survived spread out across the galaxies, ours included. And long ago, some had settled on my home planet. I've been told it was similar to earth in many ways. Not that I would know. I've seen old photographs and models, but that's mostly all I know about it.

Apparently, the founders of the Red Sun Order had been from this beautiful planet Earth. Part of the generation that destroyed it through global warming, financial imbalance, and war, they were hell-bent on continuing their reign on other planets.

CHAPTER
FOURTEEN

Back in the hotel, we didn't sleep right away. Rather, we strategized for tomorrow. Kavita paced the floor and Memory followed at her heels, beeping and booping new data and statistics about what was happening here and how we could best combat it.

That little robot dog had helped us through so many tough times and saved our asses more times than I could count. I couldn't imagine life without him now, even though he scared the hell out of me when we first met.

It was so soon after the war, and many of us had been conditioned to fear the robots. Even this cute dog could look menacing with his red glowing eyes and his mechanical bark. I spent quite some time with Kavita and Memory before I learned to completely relax around him. Now, he's family, and I couldn't imagine it any other way.

Zion was off to the side getting some well-deserved rest. He had helped us in the fight as well, and he'd been running on low rations, too. Now that we finally had some credits in our accounts, we had gotten him a huge dinner to enjoy after we booked the room, which happened to be the last open hotel room on the planet.

Literally.

So many people had been displaced by the attacks and this tiny planet only had three hotels as it was. All the homes and apartments in the city proper had been destroyed by the spiders. This was a small planet already, but the civilized parts of it were all clumped together on one side, in three major cities. With most of the people and homes in one concentrated area, it made it far too easy to wipe it all out.

I was just grateful we secured a place to sleep that wasn't on our ship for tonight. Athena was home, and I loved that life with Kavita, but sometimes the cramped quarters and constant on-the-go life wore on me. Sometimes, it was nice to sleep in a real bed, not flying through space at breakneck speed, and to look out the window and see that you were on level ground, looking up at space, rather than in the space looking down.

Bounty hunter life was perfect for me. It was as if I had been born specifically for it. But every now and then, like tonight, it was nice to step outside of it all and think about what it would be like to have a "normal" life... whatever any of us could even call normal anymore.

Not that I had ever had a normal life before then either. Maybe that's why I didn't miss it the way most did. Maybe that's why Kavita felt the same. Perhaps... it was even what drew us together. Two lost souls wandering the universe, hunting fugitives to earn a living, until fate slammed us hard into one another, forcing us to realize there truly *is* someone for everyone.

"After we help the Fire Brigade," she said, interrupting my thoughts from across the room, "We'll go to the junkyard for parts for Athena."

Nodding, I walked over to kiss her cheek, having to stand on my tiptoes to reach. "How bad is the damage, you think?"

"Not too bad. I wish there had been another way," she added wistfully.

"You did what you had to," I reassured her, and

then crossed the room to snatch up my toiletries bag. In the first few years after the way, these types of things were unheard of. Toothpaste... hell, even toothbrushes were impossible to find. I remember literally scratching plaque off my teeth with my fingernails while I hunted for a suitable replacement for months.

People had modified them into shanks or made them into tools. During the war, everything becomes a weapon. During the apocalypse, everything is useful. And most things stop being used for what they had been made for.

As soon as the war ended, the government completely collapsed. Entire planets had been wiped completely off the map. There was no work in bounty hunting, as there was no one to order the bounties or pay the reward.

Instead, I'd made my living doing rescue flight missions from destroyed planets, carrying survivors to reunite with loved ones, or to refugee planets like Strelirus. Money was useless then. Paper currency was a joke, and coins hardly worth the metals they were made of. Instead, we took payment in bartered goods and food. Sometimes even a traded service here and there.

I kept busy flying Buttercup back and forth

between war-torn planets, and carting survivors away from space stations after their planets had been demolished. Sometimes, especially when there were women and children involved, I found it hard to look at them or to talk to them.

Each dirty, starving child reminded me of myself. A little girl from Tecephus, orphaned after my mother was murdered by space looters. She'd had me hide in the storage locker when they approached, sensing they were up to no good. I've never felt so helpless in all my life as I did cowering there, watching them hurt her and not being able to do anything about it.

Zion came running as fast as he could, but it was too late to save her. We buried her together in the backyard underneath her favorite fruit tree, before they came to take me away to a girls' home.

"Yeah, but I feel bad breaking her and then just leaving her there alone like that," Kavita followed me into the bathroom to brush her own teeth. Of all the post-apocalyptic luxuries I never expected to have, love was at the top of that list. This woman had been the truest gift I'd ever received in my entire life and some days I still wanted to pinch myself to see if it was real.

"She'll understand," I said, bumping her hip into

mine as I put my toothbrush away. We still didn't have toothpaste. Goddess, it had been ages since I'd seen any of that. But they started manufacturing toothbrushes again, along with other necessities of life, about six to nine months after the Red Sun Order was eradicated.

"I hope she does" she laughed as she finished up her own teeth.

We'd parked Athena in the garage out at our property once we were certain it was secured, and we'd have to head back over and work on her before she could fly again. But for now, we desperately needed sleep so we could go help Reece and the fire squad with getting the shields up tomorrow.

"One thing at a time," I kept reminding myself. Kavita came over and kissed me on the forehead, pulling me close so that my head was on her chest. Soaking up the sweet scent of her, I buried my face in her breasts and closed my eyes.

"I love you."

"I love you, too."

Sometimes that was really all that needed to be said between us. We crawled into the hotel bed together, pulling the warm, thick comforter up to our chins.

"Lights", she commanded, and the voice-activated lights turned off, leaving us with just the moonlight filtering in through the slits in the shades. Memory had powered down and Zion was lightly snoring from the other side of the room.

Nothing calmed my anxious nerves like her. She knew how to love me in a way that no one ever had before. It was about more than the sex; she connected with me on a soul level. That was something I'd never experienced in all my life unless you counted Zion (and he couldn't talk).

As someone who had spent the majority of my life alone, this was both comforting and miraculous that she even found a way through all the armor of my hardened heart.

Lying here in her arms, the whole world could burn around us (and it *had* before), and I would not bat an eyelash. All I needed was her, and moments like this just solidified that even more. I don't even remember drifting off to sleep.

The next thing I remember was waking to Memory, our trusty alarm clock.

CHAPTER FIFTEEN

"Beep boop, four o'clock."

I groaned as Memory warbled around the hotel room waking us and doing calculations for... well actually, I didn't know what the hell he was calculating, but he was always running numbers on something.

Zion growled as he yawned, and stretched his large, muscular body before standing up and moving toward the window. He always preferred being outside. I'm sure that was the wolf in him. But he also never went far from me, especially if there was trouble on the horizon.

I'd guess that's the reason he stayed in the room with us last night. Admittedly, I did feel safer with him there.

CHAPTER FIFTEEN

The suns weren't even up yet, which was precisely the plan. We needed to install the shields up in the atmosphere, several miles out from the surface of the planet, and we needed to do it before the twin suns started rising and emitting their heat and light on us.

Although Logara had two suns, they were not as bright or hot as suns on some other planets. Perhaps that is what allowed it to create a perfect ecosystem for humanoid races like us.

We pulled on work clothes, grabbed a banana from the lobby of the hotel, and made our way out the doors. Memory came with because he was going to help with the calculations for the shields. Zion had some other tasks to do on his own today, part of which including guarding Athena. I'd told him to meet us at the property after noonish and we'd start surveying the damage to our ship.

On the way to the fire station, we ran into a familiar face. Kavita spotted him first, and turned on her heels, likely hoping to miss him, but it was too late. I laughed a bit out loud to myself. He annoyed me too, but her distaste for him was far stronger and it amused me.

"Ladies, ladies, ladies! The most gorgeous bounty hunters to fly the galaxy, here in the flesh!"

"What are you doing here Bingo?"

"I want to watch these bastards die," he snarled. I don't think I'd ever heard the little guy so angry sounding.

"Why do you care?" I barked.

Maybe I was a little too harsh snapping back at him like that, but I was on edge, and I didn't have the patience for Bingo-level foolishness today, even if it did usually bring me amusement. We had a job to do, and nothing was going to stand in our way.

Kavita stood just a step away, watching and no doubt waiting in case I said I wanted to flick him away. He lowered his voice before he continued, his lower lip trembling a bit as he forced the words out.

"They came to our planet, ya know? Destroyed everything we've been working for. The bastards burned our larvae and made the mothers watch!"

Wincing at his words, her face softened. Kavita always had a soft spot for children, even if she tried her damnedest not to show it. And what he was describing sounded pretty damn horrible.

We'd all been through a lot during the war, and even more so in the aftermath. There wasn't a soul left in this galaxy that hadn't been impacted by it in one way or another. If we didn't have compassion, that made us no better than the Red Sun Order.

"Alright, you can come." I relented, and Kavita nodded, saying nothing.

He squealed in delight, actually jumping up and down on his short, skinny back legs.

"But you have to pull your weight," I added before Kavita could say exactly that.

"Yes, yes, yes," he chittered, falling in step beside us. "Bingo will pull weight. Bingo will help."

The three of us walked from the hotel over to the Fire Station together, with Bingo uncharacteristically quiet most of the way there.

"Safari, Kavita, thank you for coming," Reece greeted us at the front of the fire station. Large crowds of people from many different races were already forming. There was a faint golden glow of the suns that would soon be making their way up in the sky.

"Wouldn't be anywhere else right now, my friend."

Bingo bounced silently on his back legs, twirling his fingers on his four hands, but saying nothing.

"And we brought a – uh – some more hands to help," I said, nodding toward Bingo.

"Ah, great," Reece pointed off to the East. "He can join the groups over there for assignments. I'm sure we'll find something productive for those hands to do."

Once Bingo was out of earshot, Reece laid out the plan for us. "We have teams on hovers already laying the framework. We could use some help from Memory here to get the dimensions just right."

Memory *booped* acknowledgement. "And we'll need a damn fine pilot in the sky to oversee everything before we activate it.

"Not it," I say, pointing to Kavita. We both know I'm one hell of a pilot, but she can fly circles around me. She's clearly the best choice for this.

She laughs. "I guess that's my role then."

Around the volunteers who had come out to help, other Logarians were gathered in small huddles. Some of them were making tea or coffee, and others were bringing food from nearby homes and restaurants.

The people of the planet had been living in fear ever since the mecha spiders had descended from the sky and wreaked havoc. For the past couple of days, they had fought a nearly losing battle trying to protect themselves from these relentless metallic creatures. But now, hope was finally on the horizon.

The plan was simple: build shields above the planet that would prevent any more of these metal monstrosities from entering its atmosphere again. At least, until they found a way to break through the shields. But by Memory's calculations, it would buy us a couple of weeks at worst, and a couple of months at best.

Odds worth taking.

The problem? Intel had already spotted a new resurgence of spiders on the way, and we had to get the shields up before it was too late - two golden suns were already rising in the sky as a reminder of how little time we had remaining to get this done.

In desperation, every able-bodied person was recruited to help with building these protective shields. They had started before we even got here yesterday. Working in teams around the clock, some collected resources while others managed to construct makeshift barriers using whatever materials could be found nearby - all against an unforgiving deadline imposed by those slowly ascending stars above them.

Finally, after days and nights of hard work and dedication, the first shield was complete! They already had it halfway up in the air. Just a few more finishing touches and we'd be able to activate it from the control panel and we'd be all set.

I kissed Kavita before we went our separate ways, and for the next couple of hours, everyone did their part to get it done. Once the shield was fully locked into place, Kavita was back on the ground, and all the volunteers were gathered underneath, it was time for the big test.

Would it work?

Reece flicked the breakers up – 1, 2, 3 – all of them activated and a low energetic hum filled my ears.

From down here, it was completely invisible. I'm sure you'd see the halo of it from space, but it didn't impede on the beauty of the planet at all down here, nor did it seem to block the suns that were starting to rise now.

There was just one more test.

Reece went into his office at the fire station and emerged with a small remote-controlled droid. It was made of the same metal alloys and had the same wiring as the mecha spiders. It functioned quite similarly to the mechas we know the Red Sun Order used during the war. If this shield held the droid out, then we should be safe from spiders, too.

We collectively held our breath as he flew it up,

up, up to the very top of the shields. When my eyes could barely make it out anymore, and the sun was starting to glare, I shielded my eyes with my left hand just in time to see the droid fly into the shield.

And then short-circuit and began to descend.

Cheers erupted across the land followed by sighs of relief as everyone realized what we'd accomplished together - preserving the freedom of Logara once again thanks to their combined efforts and resourcefulness despite seemingly insurmountable odds stacked against them.

Never had I been prouder of the place I now called home.

Kavita embraced me tightly and then pressed a firm kiss to my lips as we celebrated with the rest of the volunteers.

With one working shield in place, we knew the plan was a success. Next, everyone quickly raced towards completing another shield just in case... because no one wanted to find out what would happen if even one mecha spider managed slip through!

CHAPTER
SIXTEEN

Two days later, we were called back to the fire stations for a meeting. It was Reece who reached out first.

"Safari, the shields are working great but there were already some spiders down on the dark side of the planet before we put them up."

"Bastards!"

The dark side of the planet was uninhabited. We were certain there were some races who could stand the bitter cold that happened for 18 hours of the day there, but not humanoid ones. It makes sense that the mecha who got through went over there to hide and regroup. No one would have spotted them there at all.

"We also have another... er... problem." Even

though the phone could sense the tense tone.

"What kind of problem?" Kavita asked.

"Oh yeah, you're on speaker." Reece just laughed at that.

"I assume I always am with you two," he chuckled before explaining. "Trouble of the *official* kind, if you know what I mean."

"Fucking government," Kavita muttered under her breath before turning back to Athena's hull where she had been patching up damage for the past couple of hours.

"Yeah, so can you head over at around 0800 tomorrow?"

"Sure thing, Boss" we both responded into the phone.

The government had sent reinforcements to all the planets that had been attacked. They thought they were helping, but mostly they were a bunch of boneheads who seemed here to collect information more than anything.

I'd seen this before, in the aftermath of the war. Time and time again, I'd land on a planet to relocate survivors. The government would be there, doing pressers and promising aid on camera while starving babies cried in the arms of injured, exhausted moms who had no means to even help themselves.

Government spies with bad haircuts and even worse attitudes. And now we had to meet with a couple of them. I spent the rest of the night helping Kavita with Athena and trying not to think about what was sure to be an unpleasant meeting.

I wasn't anti-government, per se. But I had seen firsthand how they failed to help the people they were sworn to uphold. Always looking out for themselves and the system above all else. The rest of us were seen as expendable, pawns in a game most didn't even know they were playing.

Yeah, no thanks. The government could fuck right on off!

That night, I slept like a rock. My body and mind exhausted from the past few days' events.

———

We met at the fire station with Reece and some other leaders of the resistance here on Logara, as we had been requested to do. Despite getting up early and driving all the way into town for the meeting, the officials did not see fit to do the same.

They were late.

CHAPTER SIXTEEN

"Leave it to government to stroll in whenever they damn well pleased to their own meeting."

Logarians who were present milled around, chatting over this or that, and some of the fire squad took the opportunity to tidy up the place. They'd been hard at work even after the cleanup and installing the shields, helping people begin repairing their damaged homes. We planned to help them even more, once we had our ship back in proper working order. Still, we'd been putting in a few hours a day between the two of us to help.

Just then, the government buffoons decide to make an appearance.

I didn't see the two of them at first because Kavita was kissing me in the back of the room while we waited. The idiots came in the wrong door.

"So, which one of you has the dick?" One of the boneheads laughed in our direction. I felt Kavita tighten beneath my touch, but I knew it was simply restraining herself from taking their heads off right then and there.

"Which one of you has the brain?" she shot back, not missing a beat. Her sharp tongue was just one of many things I loved about Kavita. I snorted my laughter and took her hand in mine as we looked back at the bozos.

They were Crevrods. Four-legged, two-armed assholes who thought they were superior to nearly every other race in this galaxy.

"Humans... always wanting to destroy everything," he looked me up and down. "No offense."

"None taken," I grind out, keeping my face stern. I wasn't offended. I only had enough human in me to look like them, but that genetic material had held on after many generations. At best, I was considered *humanoid.*

Kavita, too. Most of us on Logara were humanoid, but none of us were direct descendants of earth. That was pretty much exclusively Red Sun Order ilk.

But one thing the war had definitely achieved was to create a strong bias throughout the galaxy toward anyone who even looked humanoid. I couldn't blame the people. Red Sun Order had destroyed our lives. They had killed our friends and family, blown up our homes, and created fear that goes bone deep.

Now, people who looked like me and Kavita were going to pay the price in the form of suspicion, fear, and sometimes harassment, too. Honestly, I was used to it when it came to other parts of the galaxy, especially the assholes we came across through work.

But I expected better from government officials, which was likely my first mistake. Kavita had accused me of being naïve before. She didn't mean to insult me; she just thought I was a bit too sweet for this timeline, always expecting the good in people and whatnot.

Maybe she was right.

I couldn't change who I was, and maybe these fools couldn't either, but that didn't mean I had to stand around and listen to them.

"Let's go," I scowl at them. "You already made the meeting late."

"There *is* no meeting without us, darling," the one on the left snorted.

"I'm not your *darling*," I snap back as we follow them across the room to begin the meeting.

By the time the planning meeting had ended, we had word more bugs were setting up on the far side of the planet. We had strategized an attack that would lead us to them before they had the chance to hurt innocents here in the cities.

The government was providing weapons that worked against the mechas; special ray guns that shut down their electrical systems, like the one

Kavita and I have but only have one of. They'd also be supplying some troops, but I prayed to the Goddess they wouldn't all be idiots like Tweedle Dee and Tweedle Dum over here.

One more sleep and we'd head out tomorrow. There was no question between Kavita and me regarding helping. That's what we were here for. This was our home. We weren't going to get those nasty bugs cause any more harm.

And once this was all said and done, we'd track whoever had sent the spiders to the very end of the galaxy if it meant saving our home.

The next morning, we rose before the suns. Memory and Zion would be coming with us. The government army had sent a leader Kavita and I were actually familiar with.

Commander Sam McIntosh.

We'd met her a few years back on a job. We had to pull a bounty out of basic training and the military didn't let us leave with him without meeting her approval first. She was a good person and an amazing leader.

Feeling grateful they'd actually sent us people and tools we could work with, Kavita and I fell into line to play our part. It was set to be a long day –

maybe even a long couple of days – but we were going to end this.

The first few hours of the day were spent strategizing, organizing, splitting into teams, and armoring up. Finally, it was time to head out for an evening attack.

CHAPTER
SEVENTEEN

With a plan, and a full volunteer army at our backs, it was time to lead the charge to liberate Logara. Those bugs had no idea what they were messing with when they came here. As much as I had dreaded having to deal with the government and their army, it was beyond a relief to see Sam there.

"All right troops," Commander Sam shouted to the assembled volunteers. "We've got a plan; we have an army - it's time to liberate Logara! Those bugs had no idea what they were getting themselves into when they invaded our home world."

I smiled at her words. She always good at working a crowd and right now, we needed that motivation to make up for what we were lacking in sheer force. She had come with a small band of troops herself, but combined, we probably only had a couple hundred people. That was a small force to challenge the mecha spiders. One single spider could rip several of us limb from limb at the same time.

But, we'd have to make do with what we had.

And making do is something Kavita and I were basically professionals at.

The crowd of volunteers cheered in agreement as Sam continued. "We know that the bugs' forces are heavily armed and outnumbered us five-to-one, but I'm confident that with your help, we can win this fight!"

The cheering volunteers fell silent after that one and I sucked in a breath. *Eek.*

"Okay... maybe she needed to lay off those odds a little. There *is* such a thing as too much truth," Kavita laughed.

Sam began handing out orders to each volunteer group while some of them prepared their weapons for battle. We were to lead a group to flank on the left side, Reece and his fire brigade would charge up the middle, and Sam was leading her troops around the backside to box them in.

With the new shield in place, it would slow (and

hopefully stop) and additional invaders. For the ones already here, we hoped to wipe them out in one fell swoop. We were risking innocent lives here, but the Logarians loved their home, and they were not willing to give it up without a fight.

The best way to get the upper hand was to take the fight to the mechas before they were expecting us. Goddess knows we'd done exactly that with many a bounty over the years and it always worked out in our favor.

Hunting intergalactic bad guys isn't quite the same as fighting mechanical spiders but some of the training and experience carry over. And our tenacity and spirit – well, that was going to be greatly needed here.

"A machine is only as good as its programmer," Kavita reminded me on the way. She would know. She was the expert in these things.

"Yeah, but who's controlling them?"

"That's the magic question," she laughed. "One thing at a time, my dear."

We hoped that we'd find the bugs in Sleep Mode. By attacking them off guard, we'd only have to deal with their automatic self-defense modes, and not a full-fledged attack.

CHAPTER SEVENTEEN

It was as good a plan as any.

After a small motivational speech from Commander Sam, we were on our way to free Logara from its invaders. Some of us on foot, some in land vehicles, and some on motorbikes. We needed to be quiet headed in, but we had several miles to travel before we got close enough that they could hear us, by our calculations, anyway.

We'd need to kill all the engines on the vehicles a couple of miles out and make the rest of the way on foot, so the spiders didn't hear. But at least they would shorten the travel time and make it easier to bring weapons and supplies.

Adrenaline coursed through my veins as we neared our target. My heart felt like it was pumping clear out of my chest. But honestly, I lived for that shit. The adrenaline rush was 80% of what I loved about being a bounty hunter.

It made me feel alive, and that was a feeling I was chasing every day.

We arrived at the edge of their camp before dawn and silently made our way through enemy lines without alerting anyone until it was too late. Foot soldiers snuck in, completely unnoticed, disabling the devices directly from sleep mode.

Some of them made little warbling noises before their red lights snuffed out.

Way less bloody than a fight with carbon lifeforms...

The surprise attack quickly caught the bugs off guard and within minutes, many of them were disarmed. Of the few that woke during the attack, it was easy enough to put them down.

The plan was working perfectly!

Maybe we had a damn shot at winning this thing after all, despite our low numbers. They say it's hard to fight an enemy you can't identify, but we were pulling it off.

With pulse guns and electro-grenades, we threw out their communication towers. Without the ability to communicate with the ones who had sent them here, they'd be in autopilot mode, making our jobs easier.

Although we still didn't know who was controlling them (or where they were located), we had to take it one step at a time, as Kavita had said. Right now, that meant destroying the immediate threat. For all we knew, their masters could be lightyears away.

Kavita and I trudged through the sharp hills on foot, taking out any foreign mechanical things we saw along the way. This is not the time for stopping to ask questions. It's a shoot-to-destroy mode, 100%.

And although many planets had gone back to mecha-tech, Logara was small, poor, and primitive in that sense. They had ships, electronics in the shops, a few mecha streetcleaners and what-not, but there wasn't a lot of cyber equipment here. At least, not yet... it was one thing we found charming about the planet.

Simple people on a simple world sounded like the perfect place to call home.

As the battle went on, some of the spiders began to awaken. The initial attacks threw many of them offline, but of the ones who remain, they were fighting mad. Memory reported that the communication link between the spiders and whoever had been controlling them seemed to be severed.

"Yes, everything's down," Kavita shouts at me from a few feet away. "Memory said no comms are going in or out."

"Great! That's a start," I shout back as I arm

myself with all the weapons I can carry. It was time for Phase 2.

Comms were down, however, as predicted, the mechas had a self-defense mode. That mode had been triggered in all the surviving bots and we were the very obvious threat they needed to demolish. Blue eyes turned red and beep-beep-booped as they locked onto their targets.

They were coming for us. But we had no intentions of going down tonight.

"Wellllll shiiiit," Kavita laughed. "It's on boys!"

Armed to the teeth, we set out to finish this battle, once and for all. We had hardly had the chance to start our new life together, our house wasn't even built yet, and I would die before I was going to sit back and let these nasty bugs take over our planet.

These were our friends, our neighbors, our community, and I wasn't about to hand it over to those stupid bugs without a fight. They couldn't just come here to our home and mine our resources, hurt our people, and take what they wanted.

Some things in life are worth fighting for. Saving Logara was top of that list for me, and for Kavita too. And that's why we didn't think twice before rushing headlong into danger that could change the rest of our lives forever.

Isn't that usually how these things go?

CHAPTER
EIGHTEEN

With victory in sight and morale high among her troops, Commander Sam gave one final command, "Now let's finish this! For freedom!"

She was theatric, but it always got strong results, so you wouldn't hear any complaints from me.

With a roar from every soldier and volunteer present echoing across Logara's fields, we charged forward toward the stronghold where the mechas retreated. Those that were left would soon be disarmed.

One shot aimed at the precise location would knock out all power to the mecha-spiders, rendering them useless. Nothing more than a big hunk of metal and wires. The trick was to hit them before they hit us, since their laser weapons could rip through our flesh like a hot knife in butter.

Gritting my teeth, I pushed ahead. Unsure of where Kavita was, all the faces were blurring together in the smoke-filled sky. I just wanted this to be over. We'd cuddle in our cabin later.

After hours of fighting against overwhelming odds, we were nearly free – at least for now. Fighting an enemy you can't actually kill is no easy task, but it was the way of war of the future. And that was something we were all becoming more accustomed to, for better or for worse.

Even if it can't die, it can be disabled. Learning to do that efficiently is key. We'd proven capable of exactly that, and it was nearly over. Memory zoomed around from time to time, recalculating the odds and spitting out facts.

I listened when I could, did what I could, but mostly I was on autopilot now. Adrenaline was pushing me, keeping me from feeling the fatigue and the toll it was taking on my body. But there would be time for salt baths and aches and pains later. Those were the visceral reminders you were still alive.

I could live with that.

On the final pass, we saw the mechas lined up, waiting for us. We had to push through this line and take them all out or they would easily repair the others and bring them all back online within hours. And the mechas had far more stamina than us.

This was our last shot and beating the odds. It was a now or never moment and we were milliseconds behind. Beating us to the punch, they began to charge at us first.

I almost didn't see the ones coming for us until it was too late.

Zion leapt into action, always my fierce protector, charging at the mecha bugs before they ever touched me. Shooting them with a regular gun didn't do jack shit, but I had brought the laser arsenal today. One zap of electricity from one of these puppies and those mechanical bastards fall over writhing and short-circuiting.

It was a beautiful thing to see.

And the government had at least done one thing right: they armed our makeshift army with all the tools we need to take down the bugs.

It was so loud, from our lasers and the electric whine of the bugs as we took them out, one by one, I couldn't hear anything else. The noise would buzz in my ears for weeks after, no doubt. Sweat dripped from my forehead into my eye and I blinked the sting away.

Nearly there.

We could do this!

It was a battle like none before. Everywhere I looked, people were running and screaming as the mechanical spiders descended upon us. We had all come out to defend our home against these robotic invaders, and damned if we were going to lose the fight.

I heard someone cry out in pain nearby and turned around to see Kavita falling to the ground, hit by lasers from one of the spiders' weapons systems. She had been trying so hard to help protect everyone else, she didn't even see it coming. Her courage was admirable but foolish at times.

"Dammit, Kavita," I screamed as she went down.

I quickly ran over to her side to assess the damage. It was my worst nightmare coming alive on the ground in front of me. She was bleeding – badly and quickly. She'd bleed out before we could get help, if someone didn't hear me right away.

Dropping my weapons on the ground, I propped her head on a supply bag, checked her pulse, and assessed her injuries. One deep shot to the gut – a couple of superficial ones on her limbs. Those likely didn't matter right now.

"Fuck!" I cried, looking around me, trying to figure out what to do and knowing the timeline was tight. "Fuck, fuck, fuck, Kavita".

"Medic!" I screamed, my voice lost in the wind and buried under the electronic whizzes.

"Stay with me, Kav," I repeated over and over as I ripped off the bottom half of my shirt and used it to plug her bleeding, pressing hard with my hands to stop the flow. It didn't do much...

"Kavita, look at me!" Panic threatened to overtake me, but I needed to stay calm for her. I needed to guide her through this. She needed me and I would not leave her. I would not let her die here!

As I tended to her as best I could with what I had on me, two spiders descended on us. I had to fight them off, but I needed to stop her bleeding. I didn't have enough hands for this. I'd dropped my weapons on the ground, but one gun was just out of reach.

Fuck!

Pressing on her wound with my hands, I used my right foot to slide the gun over closer, so that I could grab it with my right hand. Not wanting to take my hands off my girlfriend, I stretched with all I had.

Just then, I noticed something strange about one of the spiders: its red eyes seemed almost human-like as it stared down at Kavita with what appeared to be sadness on its face... but that made zero fucking sense.

"Get away from her!" I shouted at it through my tears. No one else had noticed us yet. No one realized she was down. No one was coming to help us. And this spider was looking at her like she was dinner!

No... it wasn't. It was looking at her like... it wanted something. But not like the others in Kill Mode.

Maybe the shock was making me delirious. Still, there was something different about this spider.

"Please!" I pleaded. To whom? I don't know. The Goddess. The spiders. The Universe itself.

Of course, it would take the one thing I loved most in the world. Everything I had ever loved had been ripped away from me in this life. I couldn't live without her! If she died on this battlefield, I'd take myself with her.

"Kavita," I cried, holding her bleeding would with one hand and training my gun in the weird spider with the other. Another was coming up behind it, but I tried not to think about that yet.

One thing at a time. That's Kavita would tell me. Right now, she wasn't saying anything. Her eyes were rolling back in her head. I was losing her...

It *beep-booped,* a familiar sound, similar to something Memory would say.

"Wha-?" My gun was still pointed at the spider when it turned away from us and toward the spider just behind it.

And then suddenly it began firing at its own kind!

First it took out the closest one behind us, and then the next and the next. From there, more approached and were taken out the same way. The spider with the funny eyes continued to disable its own kind, with each spider that approached until there were none yet. Just us and it.

What made it do this? Was it helping us? I needed answers, but I had no time to think on it.

I had to help Kavita, who was quickly losing consciousness. She was paler than I had ever seen her – so pale it made me feel sick in the pit of my stomach in a way I'd not felt since...

Since I found my mother when the looters were through with her...

CHAPTER EIGHTEEN

"Medic!" I screamed one more time, but no one could hear me over the blasts happening in a nearby field.

The other robots seemed shocked by this sudden betrayal of their kind and scrambled away in confusion - leaving us alone with this robot savior. Kavita pulled her weapon with her non-injured hand and pointed it at the spider, but just then, Memory ran over the hill and told us both to wait.

Her hand dropped, the weapon proving too heavy for her weak body to support. But I kept mine pointed right at that bastard. I wasn't taking any chances, despite what Memory had said.

Then, when it was only inches away from us, the spider bent down beside Kavita, pulled out one of its limbs, and used some kind of tool from its body cavity to heal her wounds with remarkable precision, as if a skilled surgeon was sealing the wound. The bleeding stopped. Her wound was closed. That was that...

It happened so fast, I almost couldn't process it. The spider had... saved her? Sure, she was gonna need hella antibiotics later but she wasn't going to bleed to death here in the dirt. Now, the tears fell down my cheeks as the reality of how close I had come to losing her washed over me.

"Kavita?" I murmured.

"I'm here," her voice barely above a whisper, but I felt her squeeze my hand, ever so slightly.

My girl was alive thanks to this unlikely hero, and nearly as quickly as it had approached, the spider with the human eyes disappeared into the night, without a single word spoken between us.

I would have said "thank you", I thought to myself, cradling Kavita in my arms. The rest of our team had finally realized what happened and they were running over to help. There was so much shouting, bright lights, and my stomach felt queasy.

I kept seeing the eyes of the mecha-spider...

Memory warbled like he had more to say on the issue, but we'd have to talk about it when we were not in the middle of a warzone. All I wanted to do right now was get my girl out of here and to a hospital.

Besides, Kavita was the one who understood him best anyway.

CHAPTER
NINETEEN

By that evening, all was still. As the two suns were setting over Logara, we had won – for now. Kavita got medical attention and we were resting back at the hotel. She seemed to have made a complete recovery from the injury on the field, which made sense based on the technology the Red Sun Order had during the war.

This probably *was* Red Sun tech after all. The question still remained of who was behind it, though. Just because they were using Red Sun tech, didn't mean they *were* Red Sun. Right?

That was one thing that had made them so hard to defeat. Their technology far surpassed most in the galaxy, even the government's, and they kept it hidden away to themselves, training it, expanding it, and learning from it.

They had built powerful fortresses guided by unkillable forces and the ability to heal miraculously from nearly anything we could throw at them. And they hoarded all this up in secret until the moment they were ready to attack.

In short, they were a bitch to fight.

So, if these spiders *were* from Red Sun Order who had somehow survived (or revived?) we could really be dealing with a tough foe.

"I don't want to jump to any conclusions," Kavita said.

"No one's jumping to anything," I said. "But I'm just saying I've never seen tech like that before. What he did for you… that was amazing."

"Yeah, I know," she muttered, rubbing her gut where she barely even had a scar at this point. "We're going to get to the bottom of this."

"How are you feeling?" I ask softly.

"Hurts like a bitch inside," she laughed. "But from the looks of the outside, it's going to heal up with hardly even a scar.

"Well, scars are sexy," I tease.

"You're sexy," she retorts, leaning in for a kiss

and groaning a bit as she flexes her middle without thinking about it.

"No, no, sit." I say, moving toward her and kissing her back. "I'll come to you."

"You'll be coming alright."

I laughed as I took her into my arms. Even now, she wouldn't let this get to her. She wouldn't let it get between us and what we had built together. And that was the one thing I loved the most about her. She always made me feel wanted. She always made me feel loved. She always made me feel like I had a home – in her heart.

"Yes. We both will," I agree, stroking her hair gently and pressing a kiss to the top of her head.

We fell asleep quickly that night, with me holding her tightly to me. Nightmares of losing her on the battlefield plagued me, but each time I woke to see her alive and well, curled against my chest, her warm breath on my flesh, I sighed in relief and shook away the bad feelings.

She was okay.

We were okay.

We stayed on Logara for a few more days, recuperating and then Kavita insisted we get back in the air. I agreed on one condition – no large bounties for at least 12 days. That's precisely how long Memory had calculated it would take Kavita to heal completely from her internal injuries.

"Okay fiiine," she whined like a little kid, and I found it endearing.

Things were getting back to how they used to be. But one thing is for certain: we'd never be exactly the same again.

CHAPTER TWENTY

The Logarians had been living in peace for years now since the war, enjoying the lushness of their planet and its abundance of natural resources. But all that changed when a vast fleet of mechanical spiders descended from the sky one day. They were attacking with an unknown mission in mind; to take over the planet and its vast resources of Labradorite.

But no one knew exactly why.

Armed with whatever weapons we could find, we fought back against these robotic invaders. At first it seemed like certain defeat was inevitable - after all, how can we defeat something that can't be killed?

Still, we had learned a lot from the war, and that would help us in this battle, for certain.

With the government help, and a strategic plan to hit hard while they were in sleep mode, we got in and got the job done.

We fought hard against these mechanical monsters, using every weapon available to us—from lasers and grenades to good old-fashioned bullets. Taking advantage of weaknesses in their programming, we created traps that would disable or destroy them one by one.

We severed their line of communication with whoever was leading them – and this went both ways – meaning whoever was controlling them could no longer do so and could no longer use their eyes and ears to spy on us or the planet.

They'd already begun some mining for labradorite. Apparently, that's why the mechas were all on the dark side of the planet. The ones at the docking station had been more of a distraction than anything else, meant to send us on a wild goose chase while the others mined the planet clean.

But we found them and destroyed their mining equipment, too. We fought at the mines until eventually there was only one spider left standing - but not for long as soon as its defenses had been breached, it too fell victim to the same fate as its brethren.

In this way, the humanoids triumphed over technology; proving once again that no matter what obstacles may appear before us, we have within ourselves what it takes to overcome them. But we all knew this was just the beginning.

Something far more sinister was lurking. Waiting to strike.

Who was behind the spiders? Why did they want the labradorite?

We had more questions than answers, but for now, it was time to tend to our wounded and broken. It was time to rebuild our cities under siege.

Everywhere we looked, mechanical spiders filled the streets, their non-functional bodies littering the sidewalks. They had come from some unknown source, and they spread quickly throughout our community like a plague. Our only hope of stopping them was to fight back with everything we had.

Which is exactly what we did.

Now, in the aftermath, we celebrated our win.

We gathered in celebration as the suns set on that long day of combat. It wasn't until much later that night that it finally hit us: We'd done it! We'd saved our planet from destruction at the hands (or rather legs) of those relentless machines.

As for who sent them or why they came here in the first place? That's still a mystery... but one thing is certain: We will find them, and we will make them pay. This was not over.

Weeks later, the president invited us back to an awards ceremony and celebration of our triumph over the mecha. Everyone had gathered for the ceremony and then a fun-filled festival after that. There would be games and music and even fireworks.

Reece was there to administer the awards himself, and of course, he wanted to honor Kavita and me. The gesture was unnecessary but appreciated all the same. Afterward, we started to mingle and catch up with Persephone and some of our other friends.

Our house progress had been delayed in favor of rebuilding the homes of the people who lost theirs in the attack, but word was they would be getting to

CHAPTER TWENTY

ours soon. I was feeling especially excited about being back here and in our own completed home.

The celebration had just begun. Children were running and playing, laughter filling the air. Drinks were poured and music blasted out of large speakers.

After the hard work of battle, we had finally rid the planet of the mechanical spiders that were wreaking havoc on our way of life. But before the celebrations could really take off, someone noticed something strange - a tiny mecha bug crawling up the wall.

"What the hell is that?" Kavita squinted, focusing her eyes on the bug.

Our initial reactions were confusion and disbelief; what was this little thing? We quickly realized it was one of those pesky mechanical spider's babies!

Someone screamed as they spotted another one, and then another one.

"Shit."

Apparently, they had been breeding on-planet for some time now, and their numbers were already growing exponentially.

So began an even bigger mission than before: find every single mecha bug in existence and eradicate it from our planet for good. They could be anywhere and everywhere – and from the looks of it, they were.

It was time to exterminate some bugs!

EXTERMINATE: BOOK TWO

Space bugs have invaded Logara, the planet Kavita and Safari now call home. They came with a mission to wipe out organic life on the planet and clear it for their leaders to move in, but the inhabitants of Logara have other plans.

Led by bounty hunters, Kavita and Safari, the people of plant Logara fight back. They win their home, but don't realize right away that the bugs have infiltrated nooks and crannies, lying in wait for a full-scale attack again.

The battle is over, but the war has just begun.

The two lovers must fight to save their planet, and then the entire galaxy if they want to keep the home they've been working so hard to build together.

We knew that we hadn't seen the last of the

bugs. We had one the battle, but the war was just beginning. Still, I was more than ready to take advantage of this little break in the fighting to regroup, recoup, and get back onto solid footing. Thankfully, Kavita didn't argue.

The very next day after the fighting ended, we took back to the skies on a new mission: a bounty on a Xandorian named Zephyrak, wanted for intergalactic smuggling. He was notorious for tracking rare and forbidden artifacts, substances, and even technologies across different star systems. Zephyrak had been evading authorities for more than two years and profiting well enough from his illicit activities to keep him on the run.

Needless to say, the price tag on his capture was a hefty one. After the damage done to Logara, we could use all the credits we could get to finish building our home, and also help with aiding the rebuild on the planet.

"Where was he seen last," Kavita asks as she readies Athena for takeoff. Our beauty of a ship had been through a lot with us. It was the only home we knew before we started to build on Logara and she was like family to us, along with our trusted robot dog Memory and wolf, Zion.

"Says he was spotted in a canteen on Lumina a couple of days ago," I read from the data card.

"Well fuck, he would be anywhere by now," she groaned, pulling up coordinates in the ship's controls.

"I know…"

"Not anywhere," Memory corrects, and proceeds to tell us just how far our bounty could have gotten in any direction from the time and place he was last spotted.

It may as well have been anywhere…

Looking back and forth at once another with the unspoken question, Kavita shrugged her delicate shoulders. "Pick one, and I'll take us there."

"Tiberius Terminal," I say, doing my own checks and balances pre-takeoff in the cockpit. This was a space station we'd been to many times in our bounty career, and it was also the perfect hub for getting information. The terminal was located in a specific part of the galaxy that meant stops for long-haulers, short stops for passers-through, and everything in between.

If our guy had been at Lumina and was now making his way anywhere else in Crescent Galaxy, there was a good chance he would have refueled at

Tiberius. And if he had been there, someone definitely saw him.

Xandorians, known for their imposing stature, are a race of large beings that command attention wherever they go. Towering above most other species, they possess a remarkable physical presence that demands respect and instills a sense of awe.

Their bodies are robust and muscular, exuding an air of strength and power. With broad shoulders and a solid build, Xandorians embody a formidable presence. Their imposing height, often reaching well over seven feet, gives them a commanding advantage in physical encounters. And Zephyrak was one of the biggest I'd ever heard of, standing nearly 8 feet tall.

Zephyrak's robust build is accentuated by his broad shoulders and a muscular physique that hints at his immense physical prowess. Every sinew of his frame speaks of his remarkable strength and endurance. His sheer size alone grants him a commanding advantage in any physical encounter, which is definitely a top reason he has yet to be apprehended.

His skin, a deep and rich shade of indigo, carries the same luminescence as other Xandorians, emitting a soft radiant glow that adds an ethereal quality to his already imposing appearance. The faint luminescence seems to pulsate with his every movement, casting subtle highlights and shadows across his features. Honestly, I'd always thought them a very beautiful people, even if this particular one was a bad apple from the bunch.

Zephyrak's eyes, a mesmerizing shade of luminescent gold, possess an intensity that draws attention and demands respect. It's no surprise he had so many loyal followers, who would risk themselves to protect him. Within their depths lie the wisdom and determination that have propelled him to notoriety. His gaze, piercing and unwavering, carries an air of authority and a hint of the experiences he has endured.

His vibrant hair, flowing in luxurious waves of indigo and silver, cascades down his broad shoulders. It is a stunning display of his Xandorian heritage, blending colors that shimmer and catch the light. His lustrous locks are often styled with intricate braids, accentuating the regal air he exudes. His bounty photo was from his last arrest, his braids pulled back into a ponytail bundled in the back at the nape of his neck. The fire in his eyes said he'd certainly murder whoever had gotten him into this position, should he ever get the chance.

Zephyrak's chiseled jawline and high cheekbones contribute to his distinguished features. His face carries an air of nobility and strength, framed by a thick mane of indigo and silver hair that emphasizes his regal presence. With each expression, a mix of determination, intelligence, and a hint of mystery can be seen, captivating all who encounter him.

While Zephyrak's immense size is a physical testament to his power, he also possesses a surprising grace and agility. His movements, despite his substantial stature, are remarkably fluid and controlled. He navigates his surroundings with an impressive level of coordination, his actions reflecting a fine balance between strength and finesse. Many bounty hunters had chased him before. All had failed.

In hand-to-hand combat, he would take the advantage. In speed and strength, he'd have the upper hand. In sheer cunning and experience, he was top of the league. But Kavita and I do not go down easily.

We've gotten worse bad guys than him before, although we would need to outsmart him if we hoped to claim this bounty. Also, taking in Zephyrak would put a target on our own backs for the rest of our lives. If he ever got out – or just decided to sic his minions on us – we'd have another right on our hands.

The risk was worth it to get a bad guy out of the community and some money to rebuild Logara.

"Ready?" Kavita pulled me out of my thoughts.

"Just one more thing," I say, walking across the ship and planting my lips to hers. After a long and passionate kiss, I pulled away with a grin. "Now I'm ready."

We chased that big lug for a week straight before finally catching up to him on Velesia. Thanks to some insider tips, we narrowed his location down to an underground smuggler bar and donning disguises, we infiltrated the bar... and we waited.

My heart pounded in my chest as I stepped into the dimly lit bar on the planet Velesia. The air was thick with tension, a cocktail of anticipation and trepidation. This was the moment we had been working towards, the climax of our pursuit of Zephyrak, the notorious criminal who had eluded us for far too long.

Beside me, Kavita exuded a focused determination, her eyes locked on our target. Memory, our faithful robot dog, and Zion, the wolf who had become our mutual trusted companion, stood by my side, ready to assist in our mission.

As I surveyed the crowded room, my gaze fell upon Zephyrak as soon as he entered. My eyes were not the only ones focused on this beast of a man. His immense figure towered at the far end of the bar, an imposing presence that commanded attention. I felt a surge of adrenaline coursing through my veins, knowing that this was the moment we would finally bring him to justice.

With a nod from me, we advanced through the crowd, weaving our way between tables and patrons. The atmosphere grew heavy with anticipation, every eye in the bar fixed on our impending confrontation.

Those who knew, knew to leave well enough alone and stay the hell out of our way.

Those who didn't, would find out soon enough.

Zephyrak turned, his golden eyes meeting mine. There was a flicker of recognition, a hint of a smile playing upon his lips. He knew we had him cornered, that there was no escape this time.

"Ahh, the Bounty Bitches," he crooned the nickname many in the galaxy had for us.

We should get that on matching t-shirts, I thought sarcastically to myself.

"In the flesh," Kavita said, coming up on his other side, opposite me.

The tension in the air crackled with electricity as we faced off. My heart pounded in my chest as the anticipation mounted, the final showdown about to commence. Reaching for my tase-launcher, I prepared to shoot right for his jugular, intent on taking the big guy down. A direct shot would probably only keep someone his size down for about 8-10 minutes, so we'd have to be fast.

In a sudden burst of movement, Zephyrak launched himself at me, his strike powerful and swift. Instinct kicked in, and I evaded his attack with a graceful sidestep, my training and reflexes guiding my every move. With precision and agility, I retaliated, striking back with a series of calculated blows.

I'd missed my clean shot with the taser, but this was hardly the end of it.

Memory, our loyal robotic companion, leaped into action, creating a diversion that kept Zephyrak off balance. His nimble movements and calculated maneuvers bought me the precious seconds I needed to launch my counterattacks.

Meanwhile, Zion, the majestic wolf who had been my closet friend and protector since I lost my mother as a child, circled around, his eyes locked on our adversary. He waited for the opportune moment to strike, ready to lend his strength and ferocity to our cause.

Zion was huge, standing at my waist on all fours and above my head when on his hind legs. He wasn't an ordinary wolf, either. He carried the magic of my old home planet in his veins. His eyes shone a bright blue as evidence. Above all, he would kill for me (and he *had* before).

"Which one of you pretty little girls do I take first?" he taunted with a deep, loud laugh. "Choices… choices… choices."

Just like the bad guy in a movie who monologues for too long, this worked against Zephyrak and gave Kavita a clear opening to fire her laser at him. She hit his right arm, which we knew from his file was his dominant hand, and then I ran in with some switch punches and kicks to his face and arms.

The bar became a battleground, a whirlwind of frenetic energy and clashes. Metal clashed, snarls filled the air, and the room seemed to shrink as the battle raged on. Every movement, every strike carried the weight of our personal mission – get the bad guy, collect the bounty, return to Logara in time for the ceremony.

But the big guy wasn't going down without a helluva fight.

My focus sharpened, my senses heightened as I anticipated Zephyrak's every move. I exploited his weaknesses, delivering precise strikes that targeted his vulnerabilities. Each blow exchanged carried the weight of justice and the safety of countless lives.

In between, Kavita launched her own attacks, and Memory and Zion offered some much-needed support. The sounds of chaos filled the air, the clash of metal, the low growls, and the crackle of energy. Patrons scrambled for safety behind tables and chairs, seeking refuge from the storm that unfolded before their eyes.

Patrons in the bar cleared out of the way, many of them leaving in fear the police would show up, and others cheering and taunting as we fought.

"My money's on the Bounty Bitches!" a voice called from the crowd.

"No one takes down Zephyrak," another returned from the chaos.

I did my best to tune them out. No good would come of it and their betting on our odds served only as a distraction.

My determination remained unyielding, fueled by the knowledge that we fought for what was right.

I drew upon my training, the bond with my companions, and the love I shared with Kavita. They were my strength, my pillars of support in this battle and always. I knew we would win, if we just stuck to the plan.

Memory had told us our odds and Memory was never wrong.

Finally, after what felt like an eternity, my calculated maneuvers found their mark. I landed a decisive strike, disarming Zephyrak and rendering him vulnerable. Then, I shot my taser directly into his jugular, stunning him. With a surge of adrenaline, I swiftly restrained him, securing the electronic cuffs tightly around his wrists as Kavita stood by making sure his stunned body didn't fall over.

Now we were going to have to carry his heavy ass back to the ship... Good thing Zion was here to help.

A hush fell over the room, the battle over. My eyes met Kavita's, and in that moment, we exchanged a mixture of exhaustion, relief, and triumph. We had accomplished what we set out to do, capturing our elusive target, Zephyrak. The weight of our pursuit lifted off our shoulders, replaced by a sense of fulfillment and justice.

No one else in this place would dare challenge us

now. Not in this moment. Not when we had just apprehended the Galaxy's Most Wanted right in front of them.

As the bar fell into a stunned silence, I took a moment to catch my breath, the adrenaline still coursing through my veins. The battle had been fierce, the stakes high, but we emerged victorious. We had faced Zephyrak head-on, our skills honed through countless trials and experiences.

Turning to Kavita, I saw the pride and admiration in her eyes. It was in moments like these that I felt the strength of our bond, the unspoken understanding that existed between us. We had fought side by side, never wavering, and our victory was a testament to our unwavering commitment to each other and the cause we fought for.

Memory, our loyal companion, wagged his metallic tail, his circuits humming with satisfaction. Zion, the steadfast wolf, padded over, his presence a comforting reassurance. Together, we had overcome adversity, relying on our teamwork and the unbreakable bond we shared.

"Perfect timing, Zion," I laughed. "We need to get this big lug back to the ship. I pointed to the limp body of Zephyrak slumped on the sticky bar flood.

Zion came over to his side and we lifted the

bounty to his back, folding him over. We had to act quick. A guy of this size would wake up at any moment and I wasn't ready for Round 2 right now.

As we left the bar, I couldn't help but feel a sense of pride and gratitude. Doing this as a team with Kavita made everything worth it. Knowing that the money from this would help rebuild our planet also made it worthwhile. There was a lot to be happy about right now.

On our way out, some patrons cheered and patted our backs. Others frowned as they paid over their losses from betting against us. The bartender groaned at the mess we made in his bar.

"Bill Mr. Lovelace. He'll pay for the cleanup," I said on my way out, tossing him a business card.

I followed Kavita and Zion carrying the bounty back to the ship and we got the big guy loaded into a prisoner cage in the back just in time. As we closed and locked the bars, he began to rouse, and curse both of our names.

"You'll pay for this, Bounty Bitches!" was the last thing I heard before closing the door to the storage bay and climbing into Athena's cockpit aside Kavita.

Get Exterminate from Amazon today.

DANCING WITH THE DEVIL

I screamed as the red eyes peered out of the closet at me. From the darkness, I could see nothing else. A shadow here or there, but it was those eyes that haunted me. Crimson, like the depths of Hell itself, staring directly at me. Waiting to do all the most terrible things my overactive imagination could dream up.

That's when my mother would come running, bursting through my bedroom door, and the eyes in the closet would disappear. Back then, she was a hero to me. The force that kept the monsters at bay.

As children, we were taught to fear the things that go bump in the night. We cry to our parents who rush to our aid, turn on the lights, and comfort us. They tell us there's nothing to fear, that we'll be okay, and that they will always protect us.

For a while, it works.

Sometimes they bring us a nightlight, special stuffie, or magic bottle of "monster spray" to help us feel better. They might say a prayer or read us a comforting poem. Soft voices and warm arms hold you close and soothe your fears. And your childhood fears are soothed, at least for the moment.

I remember how my mom used to cradle me and sing me a lullaby until I fell asleep, then she'd slip out late into the night. I'd wake up to the morning sun shining through my windows and the thoughts of monsters put away, for now.

Every night, they returned to me.

The same glowing eyes from inside the closet, hiding in the darkness. The same scratching of claws underneath the bed. And the low moans that told me there was definitely more than one of those creatures, hiding in the shadows, watching me, waiting for me...

They haunted me for all my childhood. I even started seeing them outside my bedroom, in town, on the streets, at the local market... everywhere I went, those monsters with their horns and pointed ears and tails or disfigured faces would appear to me.

Everyone else just walked right on by as if there was nothing to see. *Silly Effie and her active imagination,* they would think. But I know what I saw. And I know what I *felt* when I got near them. The way they looked back at me, staring deep as if they could pierce my soul with a glance, it seemed they could sense me, too.

Did they know I could see them how no one else could?

As we grow older, we're supposed to know better. We're supposed to shed away the childish things. We learn that the monsters aren't real. The bumps in the night, the shadows of the trees unfurling like long fingers ready to grab you and whisk you away to an unknown horror...

"They're just figments of your imagination," my mother used to say as she came in to tuck me in at night. But I saw the way her head turned when I stared at them in the store. I saw the way her hand quivered ever so slightly when she told me to stop staring and to hurry along.

And I knew the truth. After I turned 18, I felt the truth, when the monsters would come out from under my bed, and in between my sheets...

I pull the silky fabric over my head, careful not to disturb my long white-blond hair that has already been skillfully pulled up in a chignon. My long legs were already nestled inside the sheer black pantyhose and my small, delicate feet were squished into an excruciating pair of 4-inch heels that accentuated my calf muscles and conveniently rose my low-average height of 5-foot-4 inches to a sexy 5-foot-8.

Tonight's date likes them "tall, but not *too* tall", whatever the hell that means.

Underneath the red silk spaghetti strap dress, my bodice was tightly bound by an inventive torture device meant to make my already-small waist even smaller and my bountiful breasts spill over the top like biscuits exploding from a can.

"Give the men what they want, Effie," my mom would always say as she wagged her finger at me, "and they'll give you anything you desire."

If only you could see me now, Mom.

I wouldn't be caught dead in this getup outside of work but the more expensive the date, the more uncomfortable my attire would inevitably be.

Leather and lace, hair up or hair down... whatever

they ordered; I would oblige. A few hours of discomfort here and there was a fair price to pay when it kept me in a penthouse suite of the most sought-after apartment building in NYC, pairing my outfits with designer shoes and handbags, and walking the red carpets of invite-only events across the globe.

Give the men what they want, Effie.

Well, you taught me one thing, Mom and I'm doing it. Glancing once more at the incredibly view of the NYC skyline from my large sitting room windows, I put the final touches on my outfit and check my phone to see if my ride has pinged yet.

Tonight's John was a bigshot attorney from New York City. I'd seen his face on all the billboards and even a light-up in Times Square. But the face on those advertisements was not the face I saw when I stood in front of him. In fact, the one I saw would send most women screaming and running for the hills.

But I wasn't *most women.*

Spending your evenings wining and dining with people who have their names on buses and billboards was not how I envisioned my future when I was a girl, but the pay was beyond worth it, and the perks were a bonus. I didn't grow up with all the finest things in life but dammit, I was making up for lost time!

I could have anything my pretty little heart desired because I had learned one very big, very well-kept secret in this life: nothing is as it seems.

And when you have the ability to peek behind the curtain and unmask the Wizard of Oz, people will pay anything – do anything – to buy your silence.

Even more than that, I had something they wanted... *needed*... and if they wanted me to give it up, they had to keep me happy and my bank account full.

We all wear costumes.

Masks.

An outward expression of how we want people to see us, or even how *we* want to see ourselves. But underneath was something entirely different. Me, the monsters, you... We all do it, even if we don't admit to it.

My mother used to play the role of a woman who loved men, but I saw her tired face when she came home after a night with her Johns. I vowed to never let them drain my energy in the same way. As she washed the thick makeup off her face, slid the nylons from her legs, and collapsed on the couch, I saw a woman who had learned to take advantage of every gift life dealt her, but she was tired.

Exhausted.

And I wanted more than her fate for myself. Tonight, I was playing the role of a high-class socialite. No one would ever guess I was born a poor girl in the trailer park, dirty and destitute.

I wish I could say my mother worked hard to pull us out of the slums and give us a better life, but that's not how this rags-to-riches story goes. In actuality, she left one day when I was 12 years old, and never returned.

We suspected she was out with one of her "dates" and it took a wrong turn somewhere, but the police never found any sign of her *or* a body (not that they had worried themselves any trying to find her, either), so we can file that one under Unsolved Mysteries. My mom wasn't going to win any best parenting awards, but she was still my mother. And although she struggled severely with any form of responsibility, she did show me love and tried to always make our lives fun.

Some of my best memories were of her and me,

singing at the top of our lungs in the bathroom, hairbrushes as microphones, dancing around the living room, how she didn't care when I jumped on the couch, and when some of the men she was seeing would take us on nice trips or to fancy restaurants.

It fucked me up when she disappeared. I spent six weeks alone in the apartment, fending for myself, before the rent became so past due the landlord figured out my mom wasn't around anymore.

There was no one to scare away the monsters under the bed.

And that's when I learned who the real monsters were in this life – poverty, hunger, loneliness, and grief. Those would cause more pain than anything with hooves and horns ever had.

But I learned to live with that trauma, and with the monsters. And if she was still out there somewhere, I just hope she's enjoying herself.

Smoothing my dress and taking one last glance at myself in the mirror, the little girl inside looked out at a woman she wouldn't have been able to recognize twenty years ago. I was all grown up now and making my own way in a world that hadn't previously been very kind to me. Now, it was my responsibility to make this life what I wanted it to be.

With my makeup skillfully applied, my dress hugging my curves, and not a single hair out of place, I was ready to meet my date. He had sent a driver to fetch me, as they often did, and the long black limo with the tinted windows was already at the front of my hotel.

"Ready, Miss?" a voice from the hallway asked, snapping me out of my thoughts.

"Yes, of course," I smiled as I allow him to escort me down the hallway, the elevator, out the front foyer, and to the limo driver who was waiting, the door opened for me, and reaching for my hand.

I eyed him closely but discreetly. He wasn't one of them. Just a plain 'ol ordinary New Yorker, working hard for a living. I wondered to myself if he was aware of the monsters he worked with.

"Thank you," I squeaked out as he took my hand and guided me into the back of the luxury car. Sometimes it still felt odd being treated like a princess.

People in this city hardly batted an eyelash at someone like me. Celebrities and other well-to-do people could pass you on the street and you might not even recognize them. Sometimes it seemed like everyone in NYC was a VIP of some sort, but when I went to other cities for work, people would stop and stare. Sometimes they'd even take pictures. No one had any reason to know who Effie Hart was, but they could sense someone important when in their presence.

I smiled a little to myself thinking about it. Sure, maybe that was ego creeping in, but when you started life the way I did, it felt damn good to find your way to the top.

The driver closed the door gently behind me, walking around to the driver's side and climbing in himself. He wore a black suit with the coat unbuttoned. The glass partition that separated my side from his was slightly open, enough that I could hear his words floating to the back.

"Help yourself to anything you'd like, Miss. If you need anything, just let me know," he said before turning his attention to the road.

It was a very short distance across the city from the hotel to the event venue, but in NYC traffic, we'd likely be moving slowly. I reached into the mini bar and pulled out a small bottle of tequila, twisting off the metal top, and turning it up to guzzle it all in one go.

You can take the girl out of the trailer park, but you can't take the trailer park out of the girl.

I laughed to myself, the burn of the alcohol sliding down my throat. As we drove slowly through the City that Never Sleeps, I thought about the past few years of my life and how I had come to this place. High-class escort to a *very* select group of people...

You see, I held secrets that people would pay big money to keep. And I knew things about the people you look up to that you wouldn't believe in a million years. Their dark, dirty little secrets... the things they keep hidden behind the plastic smiles and the expensive suits.

And I had something no amount of money could ever buy: An energy not found anywhere else on this earth or in this realm, a resource that summoned those monsters to my closet all those years ago when I was just a scared little girl, with no clue what power I possessed.

All the riches on earth couldn't buy them what I had. And so, I shared little pieces of it, for the right price, of course. And they showed me a good time along the way.

Because the real monsters walk among us. Politicians, movie stars, big company CEOs, Presidents, and Kings. Many of them had dark secrets to hide. And that probably doesn't surprise you much (especially in regard to the politicians). But there's one thing that *would* surprise you, I suspect.

They look like you and me, but they're not. Underneath their magical veils, they are monsters from another dimension. From a world that looked like ours, but darker, spookier, more mysterious... and full of magic. Sometimes, a crack would appear between their world and ours, giving them a chance to slip through. But they could only stay for as long as their magic would allow.

How do I know all of this? Well, that's the funny part. Their magic doesn't work on me. I can see their true forms, as clear as day. Ever since I was a little girl, the monsters among us showed themselves to me, even without realizing it.

Strangers crossing the street at the same time as us, the mayor of that little one-horse town in Virginia where I was born, and even the President of the United States (that billionaire one who came before Biden).

But the older I got, the stronger my power grew, and they were drawn to it, like moths to a flame.

As a child, I was protected. They couldn't touch me. But once I turned 18, it was fair game. They came in droves to get a whiff of me, a strand of my hair, or even just a distanced glance from the one who could help them stay here on earth longer.

You see, the magical veil gets weakened the longer they are here. The more magic they use; the more power is siphoned off. The only way to recharge their magical energy is to go back to their home realm. Except now there was *one* other way: me.

A poor, unassuming girl from the wrong side of the tracks who had the innate ability to recharge their magic without them needing to leave this place. And so, we had worked out a deal. They could take a piece of me, for the right price, and my energy could give them a bit longer with their magic here on earth.

For those who had lives here on earth – especially very *public* lives – it was a valuable resource. A president or celebrity completely disappearing from the face of the earth for a few weeks would raise suspicions. So, I helped them out and they helped me out.

Money, luxury cars, designer clothes, trips to exotic locations – whatever I wanted was mine if I just gave the monsters that one little thing they wanted: me.

Get Dancing with the Devil from Amazon

About the Author

Annalise writes queer fantasy and paranormal romance and supernatural stories. A lifelong fan of the mysterious, the unexplainable, and things that go bump in the night, they've turned their overactive imagination into a creative outlet for the stories they want to share.

They live in the Piedmont Triad area of North Carolina but spends as much time as they can traveling and writing from as many beautiful places as they can. When they're not writing, they love reading, hiking/running, and binge-watching paranormal shows.

Also by Annalise

Check out these other books by Annalise Clark

Dream of the Vampire Series

Rebirth

War

Destiny

Mystic River Vampire Academy Series

Insatiable

Bloodlust

Eternal

Printed in Dunstable, United Kingdom